Romance Collection
Kathl

Table of Contents

Book #1: Dominated Behind Closed Doors

Book #2: Seduced By Their Touch

Book #3: Taken By His Touch

Book #4: The Ride Of Her Life

Book #5: Dominated In Every Position

Book #6: Flames Of Passion

Book #7: Large And In Charge

Book #8: Touched In All The Right Places

Dominated Behind Closed Doors
Kathleen Hope

Table of Contents

Chapter 1: Meeting Desire

Chapter 2: Reaching Out

Chapter 3: Innate Compulsion

Chapter 4: Eternal Longing

Chapter 1: Meeting Desire

"If that man rambles on about appellate briefs and case law during our Friday night date night one more time, I'm going to chuck my bread sticks at him!" Ava fumed as she climbed the rocky terrain alongside her best friend Liz on their weekly girl's day out.

"There I am with the lowest cut dress I could find--that wouldn't have me pegged as a prostitute--and instead of paying attention to me—or at least to the girls pushed up for his pleasure--he's yammering about how his secretary had to make six trips to the courthouse in a single day over some stupid filing error," Ava continued her rant, stopping to catch her breath.

"I swear, Liz, I almost flipped him the bird and told him to 'file this'." Liz chuckled and Ava grinned, feeling her mood lighten as she remembered how tempted she had been to do something so out of character.

It hadn't always been this way. When Ava and Michael had first gotten married, he was a handsome, caring and affectionate law student, a year away from passing the bar. But, in the four years since then, he'd become more and more preoccupied with his love for his job. At first, she had been so happy for him, thrilled that he had ended up in an occupation he was so passionate about. But then, he started coming home later and later during the week, and eventually pulling all-nighters at the office every now and then when a big case was just around the corner. But, at least when they were together, they were really together, still sharing their passions and interests, and indulging in the fiery intimacy they shared. "Oh God, how I miss sex," Ava thought silently.

The sex had fizzled during Michael's first year as a lawyer. Ava had assumed he was just preoccupied with getting himself established. So, she'd waited on the sidelines, throwing on sexy lingerie and whispering naughty nothings in his ear whenever he seemed awake enough for sex when he got home. Now, sex was a once-a-month occasion at best, and they spoke about something other than work and responsibilities even less frequently than that. She'd proposed cutting back his hours, going to marriage counseling and even a temporary separation to see if Michael might be happier on his own. But, he just kept insisting that everything was fine.

"You know what?" Liz piped up, snapping Ava out of her sad reverie.

"What Liz?" she questioned, feeling a little deflated.

"Ava, you're young, intelligent, beautiful and you have a body that most men would kill to get their hands on."

And it was true. Ava's tall, slim body and ample breasts captured attention everywhere she went. If that wasn't enough, she had fiery auburn hair that shimmered in the sunlight, a peaches and cream complexion, delicate, feminine features, and expressive, emerald eyes.

"Maybe it's time you stop hoping Michael will see what he's missing and go out and get yourself something to scratch that itch?" Liz continued.

She'd always heard that the seven-year itch could take its toll on a marriage, but at four years in, Ava had to admit that part of her was already ready to scratch. She didn't take her marriage vows lightly, and she certainly didn't want to hurt Michael, but she'd spent so much time alone lately that she just felt…lonely. Even when Michael was home, it was like he wasn't really there; his body had come home to her, but his mind remained in his office.

"Oh, I don't know, Liz," Ava replied quickly. "I do love him. Not the same way that I used to, but what kind of wife would I be to start fooling around behind his back?"

"The kind that won't accept being put on the back burner indefinitely. You're a good person, Ava, but you can't keep being 'good' at the expense of your own happiness," Liz finished emphatically. Ava nodded, not willing to jump into anything right now. But she was agreeing to at least consider the possibility that the current path her life was on might not be the road to everlasting happiness.

And then she heard a noise not more than ten yards away. She and Liz were hiking through a forested conservation area on the outskirts of Kasson, Minnesota, and the thick brush surrounding them made it nearly impossible to see more than a few feet in front of them clearly. Ava strained to see further, trying to locate the source of the sound. She heard it again; twigs and leaves crunching beneath the weight of footsteps, a few feet closer than before. Ava glanced at Liz inquisitively, but neither of them could see clearly. Having reached the middle of the hiking trail, there was no quick return to safety. So, they picked up their pace, opting to continue along the path they'd begun rather than turn around now.

After several minutes of hiking as fast as her long legs would move, Ava breathed a sigh of relief. She hadn't heard another sound from behind, and she figured they must be in the clear. But not thirty seconds later, the crunching sound reemerged, and close enough that the noise made Ava jump. And then, her breath caught in her throat as an enormous, black figure emerged from the heavy brush.

"Oh my God!" Ava whispered. "What do we do?!?" she queried emphatically.

There weren't supposed to be bears in this area; in all the years they'd been hiking here together, the worst predator they expected to encounter was a coyote or a raccoon. The bear's eyes found Ava, ignoring Liz entirely. Ava's pulse pounded in her ears and her body began to tremble in fear as its eyes roamed over her body and then returned to meet hers eyes. The gentleness she found there had her nearly as perplexed as she was terrified. The look in its eyes was fiery and the heat radiating there held her gaze captive.

Just seconds later, the bear turned swiftly and darted off, back into the brush from which it had emerged. Ava stood staring after the massive animal, and her pulse began to slow. Though in truth, her fear had started to subside and something new began to take its place as she had stared into the bear's sparkling blue eyes. Since when did bears have blue eyes?

In that moment, it hadn't seemed ferocious, but compelling, passionate...human. Maybe bears drew in their prey in the same way she'd seen vampires entice their victims in old movies. "Count Bear-u-la," Ava thought to herself in wry humor.

Liz was tugging at her sleeve and it was enough to shake Ava from her crooked wit.

"Let's go Ava!" she urged.

She allowed Liz to pull her along, and the two resumed their rapid pace. They reached the end of the trail twenty minutes later without another sound from the forest around them. Liz breathed a sigh of relief this time, while Ava tossed the encounter around in her mind. They were about to report their sighting to the information building at the trail's entrance when Ava hesitated.

She couldn't fathom what made her alter her course, pulling Liz along with her to their vehicle parked outside the gates. But something about the bear's eyes had shaken her to the core, and she wasn't ready to share any part of the story just yet. Liz looked at her quizzically, but her friend was too relieved to have reached safety to care about anything else at the moment.

The women drove in silence. It was Ava's turn to drive this week, and so she traveled the twenty-three miles to Liz's house one city over, and then returned home. Of course, the house was empty and quiet except for the television murmuring in the background. She always left it on when she went out; it felt better to return to a noisy house than one always as silent as the grave.

Feeling nostalgic after talking about Michael all afternoon, Ava tossed her bag on the living room's end table and grabbed a photo album from the bookshelf. She poured a glass of wine and sat down on her sofa. She flipped through the pages slowly, reminiscing about their honeymoon in St. Lucia, their road trip across the southwest; and the day they purchased their home. A lone tear rolled down Ava's cheek as she ran her fingers across the photos, mourning the loss of her relationship as she realized neither one of them were the people in those pictures anymore. Ava drifted off to sleep, worn out from her afternoon hike and the terrifying and odd encounter that had ensued.

Chapter 2: Reaching Out

Ava wasn't sure how long she'd been asleep when her eyes flew open. A noise outside her patio doors had startled her awake, and she was off the sofa instantly, her nerves still frayed from the day's adventure. Her arms came out to steady her disoriented body, and she turned toward the patio to listen.

At first, she heard nothing but the television in the background, but then she heard the faint sound of footsteps moving closer. She tiptoed quietly toward her cell phone in her bag on the end table a few feet away, keeping her eyes on the glass doors as she moved. A head came into view for only the briefest of moments, but in that short time she met the eyes of the stranger outside. He was gone in a flash, and Ava raced toward the patio to catch the snoop.

But, he was already gone. There was absolutely no sign that anyone had been there at all, and Ava wondered if she'd imagined it because in that brief moment when she saw the stranger through the glass, she could have sworn she was staring at the bear's eyes once again.

Ava sighed. "One strange encounter in the woods, and I'm losing my marbles."

She looked at the clock and realized the afternoon had hastened by as she slept. Ava made her way into the kitchen and rummaged through the fridge in search of food. She came away with the leftovers of a spaghetti dinner she'd made for her and Michael two nights prior. There was plenty left since he'd never shown up. She warmed it up in the microwave, sat down to dine alone and then sat in front of the noisy television all evening, drowning out the silence in her home.

Hours later, still feeling weary, Ava climbed the stairs to her bedroom. She stripped off her clothing and flopped onto the bed, sprawling out naked as the moonlight streamed through the open window and softly highlighted every curve of her body. She was asleep in moments, but she tossed and turned all night as images of the bear with the human-like blue eyes plagued her dreams.

The week passed by like any other, a blur of work, errands, housework and lonely hours in front of the television at home. She'd spent her entire Friday in her backyard, giving her garden some much overdue attention. So, when she stepped into the shower on Saturday morning, Ava sighed; the warm water cascaded over her body, soothing her aching muscles.

She washed her long, auburn hair and soaped up her body, running her hands along her soft, ivory skin. When her fingers grazed her nipples, she felt a ripple of pleasure course through her body and settle between her legs.

An image of the bear's eyes flashed through her mind. She cupped her tits in her hands and squeezed gently, all the while focusing on those blue eyes. One hand left her tits to trail downward, sliding along her soap-slick ribs, her stomach and then lower to find her silken smooth pussy. Her fingers made contact with her clit and she rubbed, slowly at first but as her arousal built, she pressed harder, moving faster. She moaned, thinking about the bear's eyes roaming over her body and her fingers' pace became frantic. Within moments she could hold back no longer and Ava started to cum, moaning loudly while keeping those eyes at the forefront of her mind as the spasms of her orgasm shook her body.

Liz was waiting in her living room when Ava descended the stairs, and she smiled at her friend as a light blush crept across her cheeks, wondering just how long Liz had been there and whether she'd heard Ava's moans of pleasure just moments before.

"Hey Liz," she greeted, feigning nonchalance. "Ready for a hike?" Ava queried.

"You've got to be kidding, right? After what happened last week, you want to go back there?" Liz asked incredulously.

"We've been hiking that trail for years Liz. I'm sure everything will be just fine."

"OK. But if that bear creeps up on us again, you're dinner, not me," she responded, though the good-natured tone in her voice told Ava she'd never actually throw her friend to a hungry bear. Besides, Liz had call the conservation area last week, and she was sure the bear would have been caught and cleared out by now.

Ava tucked her cell phone in her back pocket just in case and twenty minutes later, they'd made it to the conservation area. The quiet surrounding them as they started along the trail reassured Ava that at least they'd easily hear anything approaching them.

Liz chattered on about her newest boyfriend—"the flavor of the month" as she liked to call them. She didn't tend to gravitate toward the kind of guy who stuck around for long, but Liz was perfectly happy with her relationship situation.

"Just not ready to settle down like you, Ava," Liz would tell her anytime they stumbled onto the subject. This week, Ava couldn't seem to muster up the argument that her long-term relationship was more satisfying than Liz's string of casual affairs.

About halfway through Liz's recanting of her most recent sexual conquest, the ground began to crunch like it had before, a few yards behind them. Liz panicked, squealing in fear. But the same terror failed to well up within Ava this time. Instead, she remained completely still, listening as the sounds got closer. And then, just as before, the enormous bear appeared from the heavy brush. Liz turned to run, but Ava didn't move. She met the bear's eyes and felt the same compulsion rise within her again. She took a single step, toward the bear rather than backwards, and the bear continued to meet her gaze.

She took two more steps forward, the bear remaining completely still. Ava swallowed hard; the logical part of her brain screamed at her, "That's a bear! Are you insane?!?" But some other part, deep inside her, propelled her onward.

Ava slowly crossed the few steps that remained between them, and as she stopped less than a foot away, the bear lowered its head to continue meeting her gaze. Her hand came out and with trembling fingers, she reached up to touch the thick, downy fur of its neck.

"Oh my God." The whisper escaped Ava's lips as she gently stroked the massive beast's fur.

"Ava, what are you doing!" Liz whispered furiously.

Her voice was enough to snap Ava out of her stupor. She was quite certain that Liz was having a conniption fit behind her by now, and the tiniest smile curved the edges of Ava's lips, thinking how entirely absurd the scene must appear. But as she turned to look at Liz, the logical part of Ava's brain won out momentarily, and fear welled within her. She backed away from the bear slowly, staring at the ground all the while. But as she had begun to make her retreat, the bear turned, too, leaving through the brush once again.

"What's wrong with you?!?" Liz chastised her friend furiously as the two hightailed it back to the trail's entrance. "Are you insane?!?" she continued.

"I don't know what came over me, Liz. It was the weirdest thing. And why didn't the bear attack? Jeez, I was right there in front of it, and it didn't do a damned thing" Ava replied, confused and still shaken by her own bravery—or stupidity—she wasn't quite sure how to view what she'd done just yet.

"Weird or not, I should have you committed, Ava. Seriously, if you have a death wish, a bear is definitely not the way you want to go." Liz's anger began to dissipate as they neared the trail's entrance, and she had turned to her friend with real concern.

"No, Liz. It wasn't anything like that. I don't know how to explain it." Ava contemplated trying to justify to her friend what she had felt, but knew there was no point. Hell, if she hadn't been the one feeling the strange pull toward the animal, she certainly wouldn't believe the story.

"I'm sorry, Liz." There wasn't anything else to say, so she left it at that and walked towards Liz's Impala.

Twenty minutes later, Liz was pulling into Ava's front drive. "Do you want to come in?" Ava inquired.

"Oh, I can't. I've got plans for my latest flavor," Liz raised her eyebrows and then winked devilishly.

Ava smiled back at her, feeling a little jealous that her friend had such spicy plans while Ava had an afternoon alone to look forward to today.

"Have fun!" Ava replied, sliding out of the car and heading up the stairs of her front porch. She was inside a moment later, listening to the sound of Liz's car speeding off down the street.

Chapter 3: Innate Compulsion

"So, laundry or vacuuming? What's on the agenda today?" she asked herself aloud. "OK, laundry it is," she replied aloud to herself, wondering if Liz had been right; perhaps Ava did need her head examined.

Nevertheless, laundry still needed to be done, so she kicked off her shoes at the door and started walking toward the laundry room, stripping off her T-shirt and shorts as she went. She was hot and sticky after speed-hiking long the trail, and figured her clothes were the first order of business. Ava tossed them in the washer and then crossed the living room to retrieve her laundry basket from upstairs. Halfway through the living room, a noise outside caught her attention.

She turned to look out on the patio and froze. There was a man standing on the other side of her patio doors. He didn't look menacing exactly. He was extremely tall with short, black hair, and his muscular frame was evident through his close-fitting tee.

He just stood there, looking at her. Fear coursed through Ava's veins as she looked around, desperately searching for her phone to call for help. Not finding it, she cast a furtive glance at the man on her patio and her eyes met his. She stood motionless for a moment and then took a step forward, her leg moving of its own volition. The man's gaze held her captive, just as she had been imprisoned by the bear's eyes. Her legs propelled her forward slowly, and the movements felt familiar.

She stopped in front of the glass and the man's eyes left hers to roam over her body. Instead of screaming in fear or blushing red, realizing she was standing there in a bra and thong, Ava did nothing. She watched the fiery heat set the stranger's eyes ablaze and felt the same heat begin to radiate through her body.

Ava couldn't explain it; she should feel pure terror, not arousal. And in the next moment, as his hands came up to press against the glass just inches away from her breasts, she couldn't fathom why her nipples were instantly hard in response. His eyes returned to meet hers, and the knowing look there told her he knew exactly how her body was responding to him.

Her hand reached for the door's handle, all the while her logical brain screamed at her to stop. But the strange, innate desire welling up inside her refused to listen. It was the biggest risk she'd ever taken, and maybe the most asinine thing she'd ever done, but it didn't matter. Her body was going to open that door, regardless of the opinion of her logical side.

Ava grasped the cool, hard steel and slid the door open slowly. The stranger lowered his hands from the glass but his eyes never left hers. "Who are you? Why are you here?" she whispered, not sure which answer was more important to her.

"I've tried to stay away Ava. God, I've tried for so long. What you feel right now, it's nothing compared to the torment I've suffered watching you week after week. I've been drawn to you since the first moment I saw you, but always I resisted. I can't resist any more. I don't want to, Ava," he explained huskily.

"I don't understand," she responded, her logical side trying to force up panic and fear through the shroud of instinctive arousal.

"You know who I am, don't you?" he queried, though the stranger's question sounded more like a statement to Ava. He slowly reached for her hand with his, and brought it up to his neck gently. He looked into her eyes intently, and in less than a moment, understanding dawned.

"No! It's not possible," Ava whispered emphatically. "It can't be…you can't be," she continued, searching his eyes for some other explanation.

He stepped forward and in her confused and aroused state, she stepped backward, allowing him entrance into her home. He turned from her briefly to close the glass door behind him and then his eyes were on Ava once again.

"You can't deny this, Ava. You feel it just as I do," he urged gently.

"But...but I'm married. I can't..." her words trailed off.

"But you know this is not where you belong. Already, your body responds to me more than it ever did to your husband. Let me show you, Ava," he whispered just a hair's breadth away from her lips.

And when she didn't pull away, the stranger's lips came down on hers, gently at first. After a moment, a tiny moan escaped her lips, and it was enough to spur the stranger onward. He deepened the kiss as Ava's arms encircled his neck. Her mouth opened as his tongue plied against her lips and her tongue came out to meet his. His hands moved to Ava's hips, and he pulled her hard against him. She could feel the rock hard proof of his arousal against the soft flesh of her stomach and she gasped. A moment of lucidity broke through, clearing her arousal-befuddled brain and she broke the kiss.

"This is wrong. You just showed up at my door and I let you in. Why did I do that? I don't even know your name," she breathed against his lips, but she didn't move to pull away from his grasp on her hips.

"I don't know why, Ava. I've tried to fight it, too. But I promise you, it's relentless; this innate compulsion you feel, it won't leave you alone."

"And my name is Ethan," he grinned at his impromptu introduction as his hands left her hips then to travel upward. His fingers grazed her ribs, outlined the sides of her breasts and continued around to the upper swells, pushed up by the satin fabric of her bra. He trailed a single finger down in between her tits and Ava shivered in response. His fingers continued to tease her, grazing over her nipples just as her own fingers had done that morning, In that moment, the image of the bear's piercing eyes flashed through her mind and she looked up into those same eyes before her now. She knew then that Ethan had spoken the truth. And for some reason, that made him all the more difficult to resist. When his hands cupped her tits, she moaned and her body arched toward him instinctively.

In the next moment, his hands had left her body and her eyes met his once again, questioning.

"I want to see you naked, Ava. I want you to bare every inch of your body to me," he whispered, a hard edge to his tone as he gritted back his own desire.

Looking in his eyes, the draw she felt toward him was powerful, and she knew that she would not deny him what he wanted. Her hands reached for the clasp of her bra in between her shoulder blades, and in the next second, her tits sprang free as the bra fell to the floor. She waited, thrilling to the feel of his eyes on her naked flesh.

"Don't stop, Ava," he urged her.

She swallowed hard and then hooked her fingers in the sides of her thong. Slowly, she slid the fabric down, exposing her pussy to his view. Ava leaned forward, sliding the thong down her legs, holding his gaze as she flicked the fabric off her feet. She stood naked before him, arousal coursing through her veins as the soft flesh of her cunt became wetter every second.

"I want to see your hands on your body. Squeeze your tits for me, Ava," he guided.

She blushed but her hands moved as he'd instructed, squeezing her tits, the depth of her arousal making her squeeze harder than she was accustomed to, and she moaned, enjoying the mixture of sensations. Ethan swooped down in one swift movement and caught one of Ava's nipples in his mouth. He sucked gently at first and then stopped, circling her nipple with his tongue. He nibbled a moment later and Ava whimpered at the incredible sensation, and then he nibbled harder to gauge her response.

"Oh!" she moaned, enjoying the exquisite combination of pleasure and the tiniest sensation of pain.

Ethan left her tits and began his descent, kissing, licking and nipping his way down her abdomen. When he reached her clit, he used the same combination there, driving her wild. Her hips thrust forward, demanding more, and he happily obliged, sucking her clit into his mouth.

"Oh my God!" she cried.

Michael had never done such incredible things to her body. Ethan sucked hard, looking up to meet her eyes as his mouth remained on her body. But Ava's body couldn't take anymore, and she bucked wildly as she toppled over the edge, cumming harder than ever before.

Ethan released her clit, but he wasn't finished. His tongue came out to tease the tiny nub, and then reached further to glide along her smooth, wet lips. He teased her lips over and over again as Ava's arousal skyrocketed as if it hadn't been satiated just moments before.

Ethan stopped and stood, and Ava's hands came out instantly. She pulled at the hem of his soft, cotton shirt and had it over his head in the blink of an eye. Her hands returned to trail along the solid, muscular wall of his chest, gliding down his abdomen. She reached for the fly of his jeans when she reached his waist, but her trembling fingers stumbled in their efforts. Ethan's hands were there, unzipping his jeans, and Ava pulled them down, revealing his massive cock.

Ethan kicked off the jeans and then sprawled out on the soft carpet covering Ava's floor. His arms brought her with him, but he deftly spun her around on top so that her pussy was only inches away from his face. She could feel his eyes on her cunt, and it sent an enormous tremor of pleasure through her body. And then his hands were on her; his fingers parted her lips and his tongue plunged inside, thrusting in and out, over and over again.

She moaned, admiring the cock in front of her for a brief moment, sliding her fingers along the length of his shaft. The urge to suck his cock grew exponentially and Ava leaned forward to wrap her lips around his tip. She slid down slowly, sheathing his cock within the warm confines of her mouth. Once she could take in no more, she reversed her direction, sliding upward until only the head of his dick remained inside. She repeated the sensual action, sliding up and down along his length, trying to take a little more in her mouth every time. His hips thrust forward in response, forcing his cock to the back of her throat. The tight spasms there drove him wild and he delved deep in her pussy in response.

As he fucked her with his tongue, his hands came up to squeeze her ass, digging his fingers into her flesh. Ava moaned and writhed on top of him as her mouth continued to bob up and down on his cock. She was so heady with arousal that she didn't hesitate when his hands released her and a moment later she felt his finger pressing against her ass hole. No one had ever touched her there but her logical brain had been completely submersed below the innate desire that drove her to give this man access to every part of her.

He pressed harder and his finger, soaked with the wetness of her pussy, slid into her ass. He moved slowly at first, sliding his finger in and out while his tongue remained in her cunt. But as Ava's body began to thrust back to meet his every plunge, he slid another finger inside her ass and increased his speed.

"Oh my God, Ethan! Oh, God, it feels so good. Please, don't stop!" Ava cried before returning to the cock in front of her.

He was penetrating every hole she possessed, and that thought alone was driving her insane. She thrust back harder as she felt another cataclysmic orgasm grip her body and she screamed around his cock as she started to cum.

It nearly sent Ethan over the edge, and he couldn't hold back any longer. Before the spasms of her orgasm had ceased, Ethan had flipped Ava around and rolled her beneath him. He lined up his cock with her cunt and he plunged in all the way to the hilt in one swift movement.

He remained still, giving her a moment to adjust to his girth and then began to move slowly, withdrawing all but the head of his cock from her pussy before plunging back inside. He increased his pace gradually, thrusting over and over again until he was pounding her cunt, his balls slapping against her ass with every thrust. Ava writhed beneath him and her legs came up to wrap around his hips. Her fingers clawed along his back as she moaned, whimpered and cried out; Ava looked wild, so engrossed in innate, unbridled pleasure.

Her eyes widened in disbelief as another orgasm built. As Ethan's eyes met hers Ava's pussy spasmed hard around his cock as she began to cum. The sensations of her cunt gripping his dick sent Ethan over the edge and he groaned loudly, shooting his load deep inside her. His cock remained inside her for a moment, both of them enjoying the aftershocks of orgasm, and then Ethan rolled next to Ava, pulling her in his arms. She panted against his chest as a sensual, satisfied smile curved her lips.

Chapter 4: Eternal Longing

A moment later, Ava heard the sounds of Michael's car pulling into the front drive and she sat up in panic.

"Oh no!" She knew she wasn't satisfied with her relationship with Michael, particularly after the raw, instinctual pleasure she'd experienced today, but she couldn't deal with it like this.

But Ethan was already moving, redressing and passing Ava her clothes. She looked up at him apologetically, but he shook it off.

"We have time to figure out what this is, Ava. Meet me tomorrow…you know where." He smiled meaningfully at her and then his eyes to roam over her naked body one last time before leaving through the glass patio doors.

Ava jumped quickly as she heard Michael's key turn in the lock. She didn't bother throwing on her bra and thong, but ran naked to the laundry room to grab the clothes from the laundry she'd never quite gotten to earlier. She threw on her T-shirt and shorts and walked out into the living room.

Little did she know, Ava looked like a walking advertisement for sex; her hair mussed from play; a radiant glow highlighting the soft, feminine features of her face; and her nipples pressed hard against the fabric of her semi-transparent shirt.

Michael just stood there staring at her when he walked into the room, and Ava thought she had been caught for sure. He walked over to her slowly, noticing his wife for the first time in a long time, and he leaned down to kiss her plush lips. Ava kissed back robotically, but when Michael's hands came out to squeeze her tits through her shirt, she stiffened.

Ethan's cum still soaked her cunt from moments before. She couldn't possibly let this happen right now. She pulled back gently while Michael's hands moved to squeeze her ass, the action making her painfully aware of the wetness that had begun to soak her lips.

"Oh Michael, just let me get cleaned up first, OK? I've been hiking with Liz and ended up drenched in sweat," she lied uncomfortably. Michael nodded, squeezing her tits once more.

"Hurry back, Ava," he called after her as she made her way to the shower.

She could only hope that Michael would be asleep or engrossed in work be the time she reemerged. She stripped off the clothing she'd donned so quickly and turned on the faucet.

Staring at herself in the mirror, she watched as she shoved two fingers in her pussy, withdrawing them a moment later. She rubbed her fingers around her pussy, her clit, up her stomach and across her tits; for some inexplicable reason, the thought of Ethan's cum on her—his scent covering her body—reignited the fire he'd only recently quenched. She shook her head and hopped into the shower, allowing the warm water to wash away his scent…"For now," Ava reassured herself.

By the time she emerged from the bathroom, Michael was typing furiously at his computer while he spoke angrily on the phone. Ava breathed a sigh of relief and climbed the stairs quickly, hoping to feign a tired spell from a vigorous day of hiking. She didn't see Michael again for several hours, and when he opened the bedroom door and climbed into bed, he seemed to have lost any of the interest he'd had earlier, and he was asleep in minutes.

Michael was gone before Ava awoke in the morning. She dressed quickly, ate breakfast, and then paced the living room floor, debating whether she should be making the twenty-minute drive to the conservation area, or trying to forget about Ethan altogether. But somehow, she knew it would be impossible. She couldn't explain what had drawn her to him, but she was certain that whatever it was wouldn't leave her alone now.

In the end, the innate drive that made her helpless to resist him won out. She slid into her car, revved the engine and thought of yesterday's encounter with Ethan the entire way there. Ava was rather proud herself she made it to the conservation area in one piece, given the distraction her thoughts had been providing. She was hornier than ever as she stepped out of her vehicle and started along the hiking path.

She didn't know how far she'd have to go; she'd walked for nearly twenty minutes and hadn't heard a single sound. Perhaps whatever innate desire was driving Ethan had been satiated. But somehow she knew that the instinctive attraction that existed between them was still there, and so she continued hiking.

Ten minutes later, she heard the sound she'd been listening for. The ground began to crunch behind her and she turned, expecting to see Ethan's tall, muscular form emerge from the brush. But she gasped when her eyes found the bear who had captivated her. His eyes met hers, and Ava knew without a doubt it was indeed Ethan who stood before her.

She moved toward him and stopped just a few inches away. "Oh my God," she whispered, knowing what he was made the encounter even more sensual. He raised his massive arm and his paw came to rest against her cheek. She should have been terrified, but she wasn't. She raised her own hand in return and placed it against his fur-covered neck, just as she had before. He moved back then, and Ava looked at him quizzically, not understanding why he had withdrawn.

What she saw next was the most astonishing and beautiful thing she'd ever seen. The bear's body began to change; the thick black fur slowly disappeared, replaced by sexy, sinewy muscle covering every inch of his body. His face shifted, too, taking on Ethan's chiseled features. But in all the changes that took place before her, his eyes remained the same, staying locked with hers the entire time.

When the transformation was complete, Ethan stood before her naked, his tanned skin near-glistening in the heat of the sun, and his rock hard cock already beckoning her to come to him. She didn't hesitate. She grabbed the hem of her dress and yanked it off in one swift movement, revealing her naked body beneath—she didn't see the point in wasting time with bras and thongs today. She crossed the few steps between them and he lifted her in his arms, keeping her there as he laid down on the ground and straddled her on top of him. "I want you right now, Ava," he whispered. As she lowered herself onto his cock, she knew without a doubt, she'd never be able to resist him...and she didn't want to.

THE END

Seduced By Their Touch

Kathleen Hope

Table of Contents

Chapter 1: Hot Smoke

Chapter 2: Who's Nick?

Chapter 3: Loud Fireworks

Chapter 4: Future Date

Chapter 1: Hot Smoke

"Grandma!" Josie hurried across the yard to hug her grandmother tightly and pull her away from the burning house.

"I'm fine," the older woman said. "Just a little kitchen fire, that's all."

"Still," Josie pulled her to the curb, watching the firefighters work for a moment before turning her attention back to her grandmother and brushing hair out of her eyes. "What happened?"

"It was the oven. You know I've been saying I need to get it replaced," she sighed and leaned on her granddaughter.

"The important thing is that you're fine." She kissed the top of the older woman's head.

One of the firefighters came up to them and removed his helmet. He had dark hair, deep brown eyes, and an air of confidence and strength. "Are you okay, ma'am?"

"Yes, thanks to you, young man. What was your name?"

He smiled, revealing dimples. "Dylan," he said. "We should have it out pretty quickly. You're lucky we're just down the street."

"I'm glad you pulled me out," she said. "I should have known better than try to put it out myself." She shook her head.

"It's all right ma'am. As long as you're not hurt, that's the important thing. You didn't breath in too much smoke? Should we get you on the ambulance and get you checked out?"

"I may be old, sonny, but I'm not feeble. If I need to get checked out later, I will. Josie can take me." She patted her granddaughter's hand.

Josie smiled at Dylan. "Thank you, really," she said.

Dylan nodded and put his helmet back on. "Pleasure meeting you, wish it was under better circumstances.

"I'm going to take her to my place. I live just there," she said, pointing at a house across the street and two down.

"We'll let you know when we're done," said Dylan and turned to go back to the crew.

"He's cute," said Grandma, as he went just out of earshot.

"You're incorrigible, Gran. Come on, even if you don't want to go to the hospital, that's a lot of excitement for one day."

Grandma gave her a glare. "I'm old, I'm not-"

"Feeble, I know." Josie took her arm and walked her back across the street to her house. A cup of tea and the older woman would probably be dozing in an armchair. As long as she was okay, that was all that mattered.

Taking her into the house, Josie made sure Grandma was settled in her favorite chair, then fixed her a cup of tea and brought it to her. Josie stood at her own kitchen window and looked across at the firetruck. At least she knew her grandmother's insurance was paid up and from here it looked like most of the damage had been to the kitchen. Which meant that she'd be over here eating, most likely. That was fine, she and Josie had always been close.

Finally the fire appeared to be out. Dylan and another firefighter crossed the street and Josie went out to meet them on her porch. "The fire is out, but it's not yet safe for her to go back in."

"That's fine, she can stay here," said Josie. "How bad is it?"

"The kitchen is pretty well destroyed, smoke damage to the rest of the house. We'll get some people out here."

"Thank you," said Josie, glancing back into the house. "She's napping right now, but I'll let her know and help her get the insurance paperwork going."

Dylan gave her that dimpled smile again. "We're just glad she's fine. If you need anything else, you know where to find us. And you don't have to set the kitchen on fire."

Josie laughed despite herself. "Here, let me give you my number. She'll be staying here until we get everything sorted out." She stepped inside and wrote it down, before stepping back out and handing it over. "Thank you again."

"You're welcome. Have a good day, ma'am." Dylan shook her hand and he and the other firefighter headed back to the truck.

Josie watched them go, then went back in. Time to start making phone calls. This was going to be a busy couple of days, getting everything sorted out. She was only glad that she could be here to help her Grandma.

Chapter 2: Who's Nick?

The next few days were indeed a busy whirlwind. Josie was glad she had a job from which she could take time off to help her grandmother. They were able to go back and look at the damage the next day. Grandma shook her head at the sight, but didn't seem particularly upset about anything that had been damaged beyond repair. She always had been a very pragmatic lady; Josie's mother always said that Josie had picked that up from her. Together they sat down and figured out what needed to be replaced and started working with the insurance company.

When she finally had some time to breath, Josie made a batch of cookies and went down to the fire station. She saw Dylan and the other firefighter that had been with him that day. "Good afternoon."

"Afternoon," he said. "Josie, right? This is Nick."

"Nice to meet you," she said. "I made you guys cookies, to thank you for all your hard work."

Dylan grinned. "Thank you very much." He took the container from her. "Come on in."

Josie followed them inside and Dylan led them to a break room, putting the cookies on the table and taking the lid off. "That'll bring the rest of the guys out of the woodwork," said Nick.

Sure enough, other firefighters started appearing a few minutes later as the smell of fresh baked cookies wafted through the station. Josie was amused as she watched them follow their noses, sniff the air, and then take a cookie or two, being sure to leave enough for everyone. She chatted with Dylan and Nick, learning more about both of them and telling them some of her relationship with her grandmother.

"It's good that you're so close," said Dylan. "I lost mine before I was born."

"I'm sorry," said Josie. "You should come over for dinner sometime. She does love to cook for people, more than I do. I'm sure she wouldn't mind. And I promise - no setting the kitchen on fire this time."

"At least we'd be even closer," said Nick.

"You come over too, Nick. I don't mind." Josie smiled at him. In contrast to Dylan, Nick was blond haired and blue eyed. They were both what could only be called 'strapping': thick, broad, tall and burly. She'd buy a calendar that had both of them in it.

Dylan leaned on the counter. "Sounds like a party. When?"

"When's your next day off?" Josie looked from one to the other. They shared a look and a smile.

"Tuesday," said Nick.

"Okay then, Tuesday night, seven, my place. Anything you won't eat?"

"We're not picky," said Dylan. "You want both of us?"

Josie felt a shiver run down her spine. She met his eyes. "Yes, I do. If that's okay with you?" She turned and looked at Nick.

He gave her a smile in return. "I don't have a problem with sharing."

Josie had the distinct feeling they were no longer talking about dinner. Thank goodness Grandma would go home after they ate. Probably. "I'll see you Tuesday, then," she said. "Enjoy the cookies." She turned and walked out before she got totally lost in their eyes. Or encouraged the two of them to find the nearest supply closet.

She'd never really considered being with two men before. But obviously Nick and Dylan were close and she had to admit that being in between the two of them certainly had a large amount of appeal.

Grandma was at her house when she returned. She eyed Josie as she came in and noted her smile. "So which one do you have a date with?" she asked with her usual bluntness.

"Dylan and Nick will be here on Tuesday night for dinner. I figured it's the least we could do to thank them."

Grandma started to open her mouth but Josie cut her off before she could make a comment. "And you're going to be here, so I'm not sure it counts as a date."

"I won't be here all night, honey. You kids just have fun. I used to have fun..." the older lady stared off wistfully into the air.

Josie rolled her eyes. "Come on, let's go over the rest of that paperwork and we can figure out what we're going to make them."

"I think you already know what's for dessert."

"Grandma!" Josie shook her head at her. "Let's not talk any more about that, okay?"

The older woman laughed softly and went to the kitchen table with her to go over the paperwork they still needed to finish.

**

The next day Josie and Grandma went shopping. Ostensibly it was to get new linens and curtains to make up for what was lost, but it wasn't long before Grandma was tugging her over to the clothes.

"I don't need new clothes," sighed Josie.

"Just a cute summer dress," insisted Grandma.

"If I didn't know any better, I'd say you were trying to hook me up," grumbled Josie good naturedly.

"I think you're doing that well enough on your own," said Grandma, picking up a dress and holding it against her, then putting it back and picking up another one.

Josie rolled her eyes but let her grandma pick out a couple for her to try on. She had to admit that her grandmother had very good taste. The older woman always had been good at finding the best deals on these kind things and finding something that looked amazing on Josie. In just a few minutes she had a brand new dress, flowered, but not overwhelmingly so, falling just to her knees and showing off her curves and breasts without falling out of it.

"You look gorgeous honey," said Grandma as she stood behind her at the mirror. "They'll appreciate it. And you can always wear it again."

"Thank you," said Josie, and meaning it. She gave her Grandma a hug and went to get back into her regular clothes. She was finally able to steer the other woman to the home goods section after that and they picked out the new linens for her.

Workers had already started on her kitchen and they arrived to find them working hard. "This kitchen needed a remodel anyway," said Grandma, going past them to put away the linens. "I'm going to have a newer, fancier kitchen than you," she teased.

Josie sat on the edge of the bed. "I like my kitchen. And I liked your old kitchen."

"Ah yes, but this way I get a new stove. They did say that was the cause in the first place."

"That's good at least." Josie shook her head. "There's better ways to get a kitchen remodel though."

"True, true. Your grandfather would have had something to say about it, I'm sure." The older woman smiled at her. "I haven't really said this Josie, but thank you. I'm glad you live close by, I'm glad you're here to help me. When I do actually get feeble I'm glad to know that you'll be there."

Josie got up and hugged her tightly. "That won't be for a long time yet," she said. "And of course I'll be here. That's why I bought the house that I did. Somebody needs to watch out for you."

Grandma rolled her eyes at that, but hugged her back before stepping back and wiping her eyes, which Josie pretended not to notice, knowing she would be more embarrassed if she did. "Go on home," she said. "You need to get that dress hung up before it wrinkles, and then we need to go grocery shopping tomorrow for dinner. Make sure it's something they want to come back for."

"You're cooking would bring everyone back Grandma. I'll see you soon."

Chapter 3: Loud Fireworks

The next day was Tuesday. Josie and Grandma did go to the grocery store early, shopping for what they'd need for that night. Josie always felt like Grandma was a wizard in the kitchen and that carried over to the grocery store. She had a knack for finding the freshest produce and the best sales. Josie tried to learn as much as she could from her, but she knew she'd never be as good at this stuff as her Grandma.

They got their purchases home and Grandma got to work with the cooking, talking Josie through it like she always did. Josie worked easily by her side, finding her own rhythm that worked in harmony. Grandma gave her corrections or pointed out better ways to do things, but never yelled or threw a fit. It was another reason they always got along so well.

Finally Grandma shooed Josie off to get changed while she finished up and set the table. Josie checked the clock and put on a simple necklace to go with the dress, admiring herself in the mirror. She could only hope that one day she'd have as good taste as her Grandma did. Taking a breath, she went back out to set the table, finishing just at a knock on the door.

Josie went to answer it, smiling at Dylan and Nick on her porch. "Come on in," she said. She saw them both looking around and was glad that she'd made sure the place was spotless. She led them into the dining room. "Have a seat," she said, starting to go into the kitchen and see if Grandma needed help.

"I don't need anything," she said as soon as she walked in. "Go entertain the guests. I'll have it out in a minute."

Josie shook her head, but went back and took a seat across from them. "Grandma loves to play hostess," she said.

"Home cooked meals are always the best," said Dylan. "I burn toast, so I'm not complaining."

"Is that why you became a firefighter?" asked Josie. "They kept showing up to put out your toast?"

Nick laughed and Dylan shook his head. "I like helping people." He gave Nick an elbow.

Grandma appeared just then, platter in hand, setting it down on the table. She proudly served out the meal and everyone dug in with gusto. "This is delicious," said Josie after a few minutes.

"You helped, dear. But thank you."

"Well, thank you very much," said Nick. "And Josie is right, this is amazing."

Grandma fairly beamed with the compliments. It made Josie happy to see Grandma this happy. She knew she was more upset about her house then she was letting on, so it meant a lot to her to be able to cook for Josie and for guests.

They made small talk as they ate, Dylan and Nick sharing some stories about working for the fire department, Grandma talking some about her younger days. Josie's heart was warmed by the way they all got along. Grandma gave her a wink as they finished up and stood to clear the dishes.

"Let us get that," said Nick, standing and gathering plates and cups himself. Dylan helped.

"Thank you," smiled Grandma, watching as they took the dishes into the kitchen.

"We'll wash these, you two lovely ladies just stay put," said Dylan.

Josie smiled at her Grandma. "This went really well."

"It did." She faked a yawn. "I think I'm going to wander home. You want to help an old lady cross the street?"

Josie rolled her eyes at the obvious ploy to get her out of the house to talk. "Sure, let me just tell them I'll be right back." She stuck her head in the kitchen to let them know. They waved her off and told her they'd be fine for the ten minutes it would take for her to get there and back.

"Come on," said Josie, opening the front door and walking outside with her.

"Now do you have protection and all of that?" asked Grandma once they were out of earshot.

Josie laughed a little. "Yes. Goodness I'd think you want me to jump into bed with both of them."

"Why not? I'd do it if I was twenty years younger." Grandma smiled at her, "Okay forty… You have fun."

"I'm not telling you the details," said Josie.

"I don't expect you to. A lady doesn't tell," Grandma looked both ways as they crossed the street. "I just want to make sure you're all right."

"I am, I promise. And I'll be careful. I'll come over for coffee in the morning," said Josie, giving her a hug.

"Not too early. A girl still needs her beauty sleep," said Grandma, hugging her back and waving her off.

Shaking her head, Josie went home and found Nick and Dylan drying the dishes and putting them away.

"Well, you're efficient, I'll give you that," she said, leaning on the door frame.

"You've got a pretty organized kitchen, that helps," said Dylan. "You get her home all right?"

"Yes. Would you two like to watch a movie or something?"

"Sure," said Nick, putting the last plate away.

The three of them settled onto the couch, Josie sitting between the two of them. She felt flush, just being that close to the two of them. They found an action movie they could all agree on and settled in to watch.

Dylan made the first move. "You look lovely," he said, leaning in closer to her and resting a hand on her knee.

Josie smiled at him. "Thank you," she said, meeting his eyes. She leaned in and he met her halfway to kiss her. His lips were soft, tongue barely brushing against her lips, clearly willing to take his time. On the other side of her, Nick smoothed a hand up her thick thigh and leaned in to her ear. "Do you want Dylan, or both of us? I can bow out."

Josie broke the kiss to turn her head and kissed Nick in answer. He pushed his tongue in a bit more forcefully, hands coming up to hold her shoulders and pull her down over him. Dylan chuckled behind them, watching as they kissed heatedly. Nick's hands pushed down the straps on her dress so that he could get at her breasts, running his thumbs over her nipples.

Dylan helped her shift so she was lying half in Nick's lap as they kissed. He ran his hands up the back of her thighs, rubbing her a bit through her panties. Josie moaned and shifted so she was on hands and knees over Nick. Dylan leaned in and kissed her hip, nipping at her skin, running his hands over her skin and raising goosebumps until he hooked his fingers in her panties and gently tugged them down.

Josie scooted back, so she could kiss down Nick's chest. He moved back and tugged his belt open, then his jeans, pulling his cock out. She kissed the head and licked the slit, listening to his soft moan. It felt amazing to have both of them touching her, all coiled strength and the smell of hard work.

Dylan moved himself so that he could lick her open. Josie moaned and swallowed Nick down. "Oh yeah," he said, running fingers through her hair. Even though this was maybe ridiculous, she felt safe here. Dylan pressed fingers inside of her and Nick's other hand continued to fondle her breasts, whispering encouragement as she moaned around his cock.

"I got condoms," said Dylan, kissing one of Josie's cheeks and getting up for a moment. Nick pulled her head up to kiss Josie, and then guided her back to his cock. "You're so gorgeous," he muttered.

"Is this okay?" asked Dylan as he loosened his own belt.

Josie raised her head. "Yeah, I want this. Both of you. Right here on the sofa is fine, or we can go to the bedroom."

"Let's stick with here for now. I don't want to move you." Dylan moved behind her and tore open the condom, rolling it on and lining himself up. Josie pressed back as he pushed in, moaning against around Nick's cock.

"God you're good," muttered Nick, stroking her hair and thrusting lightly into her mouth.

Josie gave herself over to the pleasure of being between the two men. They were all still mostly dressed, and that was okay, for now. They could take care of that in a bit. For now it seemed they were both willing to take their time and draw out the pleasure. That feeling of safety washed over her again, that they honestly liked her and this all felt natural as breathing that she should be between them.

Dylan grabbed her hips and started thrusting faster. He shifted his angle, making her cry out with pleasure.

"Do it again," muttered Nick.

She could feel Dylan smile as he did it again, drawing a long groan of pleasure from her. She started sucking Nick faster, moaning and swallowing as he came, hazily aware that Dylan was coming at nearly the same time.

Finally she raised her head and pillowed it on Nick's thigh, panting. Dylan kissed her back and helped her shift onto her side, stroking her cooling skin. Josie caught her breath, then sat up to kiss Nick, then Dylan.

"Shower?" she asked.

"Sure," said Dylan, helping her to her feet and stealing a longer kiss as they made their way to the bathroom. They stripped one another and got under the spray, kissing and touching as they moved together in the tight space. It felt good to be between, to feel their strong bodies rubbing up against hers. She lost track of whose hands were whose as they moved across her body. She had both their cocks in hand, pulling soft moans from them as they grew hard again.

Nick fumbled and got the water shut off, leading the way back out of the shower. He quickly toweled off Josie and once they were all a little more dry they made it into her bedroom and landed in a pile on her bed. Nick found the lube and coated his fingers, pressing into her ass. "Can we both fuck you at the same time?"

"Sounds excellent to me," moaned Josie as Dylan pressed his own fingers back into her pussy.

"Just relax, " said Nick, mouthing her throat and holding her against his chest. Dylan's tongue flicked over her nipples. She groaned happily, uncertain what to do with her hands, but settling for one on Nick's neck behind her and the other on Dylan's shoulder in front of her.

When he deemed her ready, Nick pushed Dylan onto his back. He grabbed a condom and rolled it on, got settled, and guided her over his hips.

Josie moaned as she slid down on his thick cock again, still wet and lose from before and the heavy petting in the shower. Dylan pulled her down for a kiss and she heard Nick tear open another condom and move behind her.

Dylan groaned into her mouth as Nick pressed into her. Josie moaned in response, shifting her hips as she adjusted to the two of them inside of her. "So full," she muttered.

"You feel so good," whispered Nick, starting to thrust. She groaned and relaxed in their arms. Dylan smiled at her and she closed her eyes, focusing on the sensation and the pleasure. Dylan's fingers rubbed her clit, making her gasp, trembling at the pressure and how close she was to another orgasm.

"Go ahead, come for us," said Dylan touching her more and pulling her into a deep kiss. Josie moaned and let go, shaking and squeezing around them both.

"Shit," muttered Nick, moving a little faster. "I'm so close already."

He gave a few more thrusts and she felt as he came, deep inside of her. Panting, he carefully pulled out after a moment and went to bin the condom. Dylan grabbed her and rolled her over, fucking hard into her until he came himself, kissing her through it. He pulled out just as carefully. Nick was there, wiping her up with a warm rag and laying down on one side of her, kissing her slowly.

Dylan returned and pulled the blankets over them, curling up on her other side, and smoothing a hand down her skin. Josie turned her head and kissed him, then settled down between them, smiling softly. They fell asleep, just like that, with one on either side.

Chapter 4: Future Date

Josie woke in the morning, still tangled up in the sheets and between Nick and Dylan. She smiled and carefully extricated herself, throwing on a robe and going to make coffee. Dylan appeared a few moments later. "I'll make breakfast," he announced, stealing a kiss from her and grabbing the ingredients for pancakes.

Nick showed up a few moments later, sniffing at the coffee and sleepily taking a cup and his own kiss.

Dylan chuckled. "Nick isn't a morning person."

"It's inhuman to be that cheerful without coffee," grumbled Nick.

"This inhuman is making you pancakes, so you can stop complaining any time," he said good naturedly.

Nick sipped his coffee and stared into the middle distance. Josie shook her head at the pair of them. "Well I'm glad you stuck around," she said honestly.

"We wouldn't just cut and run. Besides, we both like you," said Dylan, stirring a bowl in his hands.

Nick gave a grunt of assent.

"Wouldn't mind doing this again either," said Dylan, giving her that dimpled smile.

"I… could possibly be convinced of that," she answered, walking over and kissing Dylan, then Nick.

"Next week maybe?" asked Dylan.

"I'll give you a call," said Josie. "Which isn't a no, by the way. I just have to see what my schedule is like next week."

"Yeah, I understand. And if we get a call to work, you understand."

"Yep, totally."

Josie sipped her own coffee and soon enough Dylan had a big plate of pancakes for all of them. Nick gradually woke up as he ate and drank, even giving her a smile as he finished. Dylan moved to go do the dishes and Josie stopped him. "You've done more than enough dishes. I appreciate it, but I've got it." She leaned up and kissed him.

"Well, if you insist I shouldn't argue." He headed to the bedroom to get dressed.

Nick wrapped his arms around her from behind. Josie turned in his grasp and kissed him too. "I did enjoy both of you," she said.

"I know. Dylan and I are good friends. We don't mind sharing. And I look forward to the next time we meet. For a few reasons." He kissed her throat and Josie shivered.

Nick let go and also headed back to get dressed as Dylan was coming back out. He handed Josie a bit of paper. "That's my number and Nicks, in case you need anything. Cat out of a tree, or something."

"Right...I'll call you if my... pussy needs taken care of." She winked and then covered her face. "I'm sorry, that was horrible."

Dylan laughed, tilted her chin and kissed her. "I've heard worse, trust me."

Nick had come out by then. They both gave her one more kiss and headed out. Josie went to get dressed herself and take a quick shower before going to tackle the dishes. She was whistling to herself as she washed up. There was a knock on the door.

Knowing who it was, she went to answer it. "You know you can always come in, Grandma."

"I didn't know if you'd still have company. And you said you'd come over for coffee," she said, looking around.

"They left already," said Josie, getting her a cup of coffee. "Sorry, Dylan made pancakes. And yes we had fun, and yes we might be getting together again next week."

"That's my girl," smiled Grandma.

Josie rolled her eyes. "Just tell me you didn't set things on fire on purpose just to snag me a boyfriend, or two."

"The thought hadn't even crossed my mind. I won't complain though. And I'm not cooking dinner again next week. You kids just have fun without Grandma around."

Laughing, Josie kissed the top of her head. "You're ridiculous, you know."

"Maybe, but, that's just how it's going to be. I'm too old to grow up now." Grandma had a twinkle in her eye.

Josie finished the dishes and sat across from her. "I want to be just like you when I get older, you know that?"

Grandma smiled warmly at her. "That means a lot to me. You're a good woman, Josie, and I'm proud of you."

"Even if I just entertained two gentleman for an evening?" she asked.

"Especially because of that. Makes me proud."

Josie shook her head at her Grandma. "Come on, I know you needed to get some more shopping done today. Let's head out and get that taken care of."

"Okay." Grandma went to wash up her cup in the sink.

They pulled out of the driveway a few minutes later and went past Grandma's house. There was still damage visible from the street, but a lot more good had come out of that mishap than bad, and Josie wasn't going to complain any time soon. Maybe she'd even bake Dylan and Nick and the rest a few more cookies, just because.

THE END

Taken By His Touch
Kathleen Hope

Table of Contents

Chapter 1: The Meeting

Chapter 2: A Romantic Re-Do

Chapter 3: The Question, and the Confession

Chapter 1: The Meeting

My mother had been looking out the window for hours, pacing back and forth, when finally the tan Buick La Saber pulled into the driveway that was in front of our tiny home. Her new boyfriend stepped out and I could tell that he looked just like all of the other pieces of garbage that she had come to the house while I was growing up, but this one was different. Buck and his son were coming to live with us. They were here to be a permanent fixture in our lives. My mother had gotten married to Buck while I was at college and I couldn't be angrier at her for the betrayal. Before I had gone to college she was my best friend. We talked about everything from what we got in the mail to our deepest darkest thoughts and feelings. She fed me some lie about not wanting to bother me while I was taking finals. My mother hadn't told me much about his son either, but I knew that he was five years older than me and went to the same college as I had. As Buck got out of the car I could tell that he had been a little drunk. He stood with his short legs and his peppered hair with a cigarette hanging out of his thin straight mouth. He pulled up his jeans that were sagging past his waist and straightened out his leather jacket before coming up to our door.
"I mean it Joey. Be sociable. You're going to love your stepbrother." My mother said to me and I rolled my eyes back

at her and looked back down at my book. I knew when Buck had come into the house by the pungent smell of Eagle 20's. It overwhelmed me and churned my stomach as I tried to focus on the words rather than throwing up in my mouth. "Buck, this is my daughter Joey." Buck looked at me and simply motioned at me with his chin. "Where's your son?" My mother asked, looking behind Buck.

"Ryan's outside grabbing our things." He responded past an unlit cigarette. "Here he is." He announced as Ryan came through the door. The smell of cheap smokes was overtaken by the obnoxious smell of too much aerosol cologne.

"Hi Ryan. This is my daughter Joey. You two go to the same college." My mother said awkwardly hugging him. Everyone in the small town of Cedar City went to the same college. Our school district wasn't impressive enough to get its graduates into anywhere else.

"Oh yeah. You're in my government class. How you doing Joey?" He asked with his deep voice, smiling.

    I looked back at him and my stomach dropped. He was tall and wore a black sweater and dark jeans. His eyes were dark jade green and his facial hair was just as dark and just as well maintained as his perfect head of hair. He was undeniably handsome and had a timelessly handsome face. His chin was strong and square. All at once, I recognized him. Ryan Lowe was my new stepbrother? The most popular and narcissistic guy in my school is moving into my house. I had never spoken to him, but I knew his type and that was enough. He was the jock who only graduated because of the small town mentality that revolved around sports. He then was given scholarships so that he could play football in College and make Cedar City proud.

"I'm okay." I responded, looking back down at my book.

Buck grabbed my mother and whispered something in her ear before they both giggled and went into her room. I had no idea what attracted a woman that was as beautiful as my mother to such scum. Helena White was young, having had me at only sixteen, twenty years ago. She had long brown hair with big round brown eyes and a sweet sense of humor. She had high cheek bones and a dainty body. She really was lovely. Ryan whispered something under his breath and came over to sit next to me on the couch.

"What are you reading?" He asked awkwardly.

"Hamlet." I responded.

"For fun?" He asked with a laugh under his breath.

"No? Miss. Pacheco told us to read it over Spring Break. Aren't you in her class?" I asked hoping he'd drop it.

"Oops." It was all he said about his forgotten assignment. "Do you want to go to a party tonight?" He asked changing the subject.

I thought to myself about how it would be the perfect way to get back at my mother for again trying to replace my father and also not telling me that I got a new stepdad and step brother. I thought back to when my birth father had finally contacted me. I couldn't find a reason why she would have taken me and left him. He was handsome, smart and kind. He told me about how he got remarried five years after my mother had abandoned him. He had two new daughters and a son. They were my siblings and I had only ever seen pictures of them. It was the one thing that my mother had always refused to talk to me about. I shook the tears from my eyes and nodded.

"Sure. I'll go." I said.

"You'll need to change." He said before standing up and taking his bags into what was supposed to be his room. The room that was now Ryan's was once my favorite room in the house. The room used to hold all of the things my mother and I had used for photography. We had both loved taking pictures of flowers and sunsets simply just to do it. Now all those things were just tossed in the basement.

  I looked down at myself and agreed with him. My green tank top and grey sweats probably weren't the best clothes for a party. I stood up and walked into my room at the back of the house and dug through my clothing. I decided on a short black cocktail dress that my friend Samantha had left in my room one night after she had gotten too drunk to go home. I looked at myself in my full length mirror and I still looked pitiful. My long brown hair looked plain, limp and dull. I turned on my curing iron and began to trace my brown eyes with a black eyeliner. Besides burning myself a few times with the iron, I was happy with what turned out. My thin body was impressive in the tight black bandage dress. My hips stuck out and were defined by my legs that were toned a lengthened by the high heels. I spun and looked at my perky round butt and couldn't help but smile.

"Wow." Ryan said as he stood in the doorway.

I shot him a glance and sat down on my bed to put on bracelets my dad have given me before he left on our last meeting. My stomach clenched as I felt him staring at me. I wished for anything to break the awkward silence as he eyed my body from head to toe. He acted like he had never seen a woman before me. I knew that wasn't how he felt, having seen him stick his tongue down Mandy Russ's throat during one entire hour long class of government.

"We can take my jeep." I finally said as I stood up.

"Yeah, okay." He said watching me pass him on my way out.

I started up the jeep and waited for him to get in. He began to direct me to his friend's house on the other side of town. He spent most of the ride looking between my legs. I did all I could to keep them closed and keep my dress down. I felt that at any moment he was going to put his massive hand between my legs. I felt myself grow wet and tense as the thought passed my mind.

"This is it." He said interrupting my fantasy as he pointed to a small white house. There were tons of cars parked out front of the house and I did what I could to park my jeep in a safe spot. Ryan got out and opened my door for me before he ran off with his friends. I should have known that this was a horrible idea. I'm not a sociable person, and just being in a situation like this one began to give me anxiety. I like to hide in my dorm and read or draw, but I have found myself in a situation that's outside of my realm of comfort. I think about getting back into my jeep and heading home when I hear a loud girlish slurred voice call my name.

"Joey!" Samantha screamed before hugging me. "I can't believe you're here! And in my dress."

    Samantha had tried for months to get me out of the house and into a party like this one. I had always denied her, but I was always there for her when she came stumbling into my house needed to sleep off her drunk. She held onto me before she kissed me on the cheek and drug me into the loud house. People rushed past me screaming and yelling at their buddies. I looked around for Ryan only to find him on the couch with some random blonde playing tonsil hockey. What a pig. Samantha grabs my hand and tugs me further into the house into a back room. A large group of people sat around an empty wine bottle, obviously all of them had been the ones to finish the wine that was once inside. A girl spun the bottle and the end pointed to some random guy who I didn't know. He then pressed an app on his phone.

"Ten minutes!" He said as he stood and grabbed her hand as they went into the next room. Ten minutes later they reemerged. Ryan followed them in and sat down. He motioned me to sit down next to him and Samantha forced me to. The next girl to spin the bottle was Samantha. Her spin landed on a girl and the same guy as before took out his smart phone and reopened the 'spin the bottle' app on his smart phone.
"Kiss." He said.

The two girls leaned in and Samantha kissed her deeply. All of the guys around the group cheered as they did. Samantha gave me the bottle and I spun it. I hoped it would land on me and I could skip my turn. Instead, it landed on Ryan. He smiled at me and winked as the guy pressed his phone.
"Twelve hours in heaven you two." The guy said as everyone else in the group whooped. Ryan grabbed my arm and took me into the separate room. As Samantha locked the door behind us.
"I'm not having sex with you." I said before he could say anything.
"We can talk." He said.
"What do you want to talk about?" I asked him. "How about we talk about this. Did your father tell you they got married?" I asked feeling irritated.
"No." He said looking down at his shoes. "Since my mom died he never tells me anything." I wish I could have eaten my

words. At least I knew that my father was alive and well. His mother was gone.

"How did she die?" I asked sitting next to him and putting my hand on his.

"Cancer." He said shortly before laying back on the bed. "I was fifteen. Afterward my dad got hooked on a bunch of drugs and started drinking. He lost the job he had as an estate agent and everything got worse from there."

"Why are you telling me this?" I asked confused at his sudden need to divulge his innermost thoughts.

"A few reasons." He said. "One, because I see the way you look at me. Like I'm some stupid misogynistic jerk. And secondly because you're my step sister now. And lastly, you have a right to know about the guy who's living in the next room." I had to agree with him. "Tell me about yourself."

"Well, my mother took me from my father when I was young. She's always done her best to make things fit together. She worked two jobs and always came home to take care of me at the end of her shift. She never let me go without. Actually, she's the only reason I'm in college." He smiled his flawless smile at me and nodded.

"Okay, so what was with the look you gave my dad?" He asked having seen the smirk.

"Well, she been bringing men in and out of my life since I could remember. In her mind I've always needed a father." I said honestly. He deserved to know me too. I changed the subject. "How'd you get into college?"

"Scholarships and grants." He said. I was embarrassed when he saw the surprise that doused my face. "I'm not stupid Joey. I just like to be around my friends and have a good time. I like to get out of the house." He defended. I nodded but didn't say anything. I just looked at him. He was so handsome, but a look of grief sat behind his green eyes.

"I'm sorry I was rude to you." The words slipped from out of my mouth.

"That's okay Joey. I get it." He reached for my hand and pulled me down onto the bed with him and he kissed me slowly on the lips. I wanted to pull away and scream at him but I couldn't. He tasted like honey and stuck to my lips. He grabbed my waist and kissed me deeper. I tried to pull away as his hand fell lower. My heart raced and I felt the rush of doing something terrifically taboo.

"Ryan stop." I finally said when he pulled away to kiss my neck.

"I'm sorry. You're just so beautiful." He said pushing my hair out of my face.

"I've never done anything." I admitted, embarrassed.

"I'll be gentle." He said pulling me toward him and kissing me deeper. "You're safe with me." I was overcome with the feeling of truly being safe and secure in his arms.

He rolled me over so I was under him. He relentlessly kissed me and played with my hair. He undressed me and himself between kisses. His skin was warm on mine and I was so intoxicated by him. I was completely covered in goose bumps and I could feel his warm breath on my neck. He began and looked into my eyes as her entered me. I felt no pain, only the sensation of fullness and completeness as he went on. I felt like it had lasted hours when he stopped and kissed me. "That was amazing." He said as he ran his fingers lightly against my skin. I was lost for words and filled with equal parts of love and repugnance. He was by all rights my step brother. He was also a handsome and sexy man whom wanted me. I was utterly torn between the two feelings.

He stood up, still nude and took my hand. He led me into the bathroom without saying a word. Inside the bathroom was a huge Jacuzzi and he began to run me a bath. He added bubbles and helped me in. He slid in behind me and took the loofa to my arms and back. The water was warm and soothing against my skin as he slowly rubbed soap onto it. I noticed for the first time that I hadn't heard anyone from the party outside of the room. I laid back into Ryan and he held me as he kissed my neck.

"You smell like summer." He said slowly rinsing me off.

I turned my head and kissed him and he returned it with passion and lust. He picked me up out of the bath and dried me gingerly with a long towel before wrapping me up and carrying me into the bedroom. He placed me under the covers and warmed me up before lying next to me. He looked into my eyes as I slowly fell into a deep sleep. When I woke up, he was lying next to me. His eyes were moving under his heavy eye lids and his breath was fast. I stood up, carefully trying not to wake him up as I dressed myself. I couldn't help but look at him and feel swooned. He was breathtaking and I had never felt so close to another person like I had with him. He was utterly gorgeous and he knew all of the right things to say. His emerald eyes slowly opened as I sat back onto the bed to place my shoes back on my feet.

"Hey gorgeous. Where are you going?" He asked.

"Home." I said feeling short and irritated.

He stood up and stretched before standing up. His tall body lengthened as he did so. His abs flexed and I had to look away. Last night had been such a rush, but now I felt so dirty and used. I wasn't sure if it was because it was my first time, or if it was my first time with my step brother. I felt a lump grow in my throat and I wanted to cry. He grabbed me from behind and hugged me. He breathed into my neck and began to kiss it again before he told me he was sorry. He dressed himself as he walked me back out to my jeep. When we got home my mother wanted to scream at me but Buck was right there,

interrogating Ryan. I walked past them and locked myself in my room. I laid on my bed and curled into the smallest ball possible before crying. I wished I could go back last night and take everything back. When I woke up, Ryan was sitting next to me. He was rubbing my back and tickling me.
"I'm sorry you don't feel well. Your mom wants to start a garden before we go back to school." He said as he looked at me and felt my head. I pulled away from him.

"I don't want to go. I'm sick."

"Sick of me?" He asked.

"A little." I admitted.

"Let's talk about it then. Why are you mad at me?"

"I didn't want to do what we did last night. I wanted it to be different. Romantic. You know, candles and rose petals. Not some house party." I confessed.

"I'm so sorry Joey. Please forgive me." He kissed me on the nose and helped me up.

We walked out into the garden and began to till up the dirt. We planted sweet peas and marigolds in the crisp spring sun.

He threw pieces of dirt at me and laughed when I sprayed him with the hose. When my mom and Buck went back into the house he laid his hand on my back and kissed me before spraying me and drenching my entire body.

"I noticed you have a trampoline out back. Do you want to sleep on it tonight and look up at the sky?" He asked.

"Okay." I said with hesitation.

Chapter 2: A Romantic Re-Do

  That night Ryan told me to cover my eyes as he led me into the back yard. When he told me to open them, a feeling of warmth overwhelmed me. He had covered the trampoline in roses. He had lit the outdoor fire place and had candles sitting on the patio leading to the trampoline. He had laced Christmas lights through the birch trees that were still young. The scene looked like it was out of a romance movie. The sky was cloudless and the stars were twinkling brightly. The air smelled of the flowers we had planted earlier. My face turned red and I could hear him holding his breath.

"Ryan." I said.

"I wanted to make it right." He answered as he carried me to the trampoline.

  He kissed me as he laid me down. The springs squeaked and we bounced as he began. I couldn't help but laugh. He laid next to me after we had finished. He flashed me a cocky smile and pointed up. We looked at the sky and pointed out constellations to each other. He told me about how the big dipper was his favorite because he could always find it. Then I pointed the Milky Way out to him and told him about how my mother would say that god spilled milk one day in the sky. He

laughed and told me about how his mother told him lightning storms were the gods bowling. We both laughed until it got cold. Ryan went in and came back out with an arm full of sleeping bags and pillows. He threw them on the trampoline and began to jump with them all on top on me. The bedding went everywhere and I laughed hard as he bounced. He landed on his stomach and crawled next to me.
"Come live with me." He said.
"What?" I asked shocked.
"My old roommate moved out, I need a new one. I want it to be you." He said as he played with my hair.
"Okay." I said a bit perturbed.

  He laid next to me and swooped me into his arm as he kissed my cheek. He tucked me into the blankets and held me as he told me stories about how he had grown up. The night air was cool and smelled of someone having a late night barbeque. The feeling that pulsed through my veins was indescribable. I felt loved and loving all at once and to the fullest extent. I fell asleep in Ryan's arms and woke up sweating in the son. I shook Ryan.
"We need to pack." I said as I inched my way off of the trampoline.

  I stood at the side of my bed and filled up my suitcase. I thought about what it would be like to live with Ryan when my mom cleared her throat at the threshold of my door.

"We need to talk Joey." She left my doorway and my heart jumped into my throat. I couldn't breathe. She had to know about Ryan and me. There was no other reason for her to want to talk to me. I followed her into my room. Buck and Ryan were sitting on the couch, also talking. I walked past them and my mother closed the door behind me when I entered her room.

"Sit down honey." She said and I followed her direction. Sitting on the side of the bed. "I feel like I haven't seen you at all this break. What have you been up to?" She said asking as she straitened her son dress while sitting on the bed.

"Not much." I said feeling my heart in my throat.

"Well. I know you've been spending a lot of time with Ryan. I told you that you would like him didn't I?" My face was bright red I knew it by the burn in my cheeks.

"I know mom. You were right." I readied myself to explain everything to her, but she interrupted me. "Joey, I wasn't around to tell you what had happened between your father and I. Buck convinced me that you deserved to know." My eyes grew wide and I was rushed with a different anxiety.

"Okay mom." I said swallowing. I couldn't believe that she was about to tell me what I had been asking her for years.

"You already know that I was only sixteen when I got pregnant with you, and your dad was only eighteen. Your grandparents forced us to move in together and live with them. It was so hard for me knowing that I was hindering your father's future.

At the time, he was supposed to be on his way to law school. He had a full ride academic scholarship and he was about to lose it. My parents were planning a wedding for us when I ran away. I left him and took you here. I got my first job as a housekeeper and was overwhelmed quickly with how much money I had needed just for us to get by. That's when I started dating. Your father was already in law school and dating a woman who was becoming a family lawyer. I will always love your father, but loving someone doesn't always mean being with them."

"How can you say that you ruined his life when it was me? It was my birth that ruined both of your lives!" I screamed at her as I ran out of the house. The pain cut deep.

Ryan yelled after me and got into the jeep with me. We drove for miles without either of us saying a word. He took his phone out and sent my mother a message saying that I was okay. It made me want to scream at him. If I weren't alive, she would have had a great life. Her and my father would probably would have been together, she wouldn't have had to work so hard.

"Do you want to talk about it?" Ryan asked quietly.

"I ruined her life." I said behind tear filled eyes. He was quite for a moment.

"Don't you think that she feels the same way? He asked.

"What?" I said pulling over.

"Joey. Don't you think your mother feels like she ruined your life?" Everything he said made sense.

"I wouldn't have traded my life for anything." I said behind tears.

"I think that's how she feels too. You two love each other." He said while rubbing my back. I nodded and he kissed my cheek.

"What was your father talking to you about?" I asked.

"He told me to take care of you and respect you. You know, now that you're my sister. He's not so bad Joey, if you give him a chance." I nodded. I turned around and drove back to the house. I pulled into the driveway to see my mom and Buck on the stoop. She was crying and she stood as I pulled in. When I got out she hugged me tightly and kissed my head. I told her I was sorry and she said that she was too. When she let me go, I walked over to Buck and hugged him. My mother must have asked him to stop smoking because he only smelled like laundry detergent. He hugged me back tightly before saying that he was going to fire up the barbeque. My mother, Ryan and I sat at the patio table, waiting for Buck to bring us the burgers.

"He's a little rough around the edges, but he's a really wonderful guy." She said about Buck. "When he's nervous he smokes like a freight train and he can't say a word." She laughed. Suddenly that first day made sense to me and I felt guilty for judging him.

Buck brought the burgers over and they looked amazing. He had cooked them to perfection and had added pastrami and mushrooms, just the way I liked them. I knew he had asked my mother. We laughed until the warm spring day became a fresh spring night. My mother excused herself to clean up the dishes and Buck, Ryan and I talked about what was in the news lately. We also talked about Hamlet and Buck told us how it ended after we both realized that we hadn't read it. We made plans to head back to college in the morning. Buck headed off to bed and Ryan and I continued to talk for another hour.

"We have an early morning." He said kissing my forehead. He took me to my room and put me in bed.

Chapter 3: The Question, and the Confession.

The next morning I said goodbye to my mother and Buck after she made us breakfast. She and I cried while Buck and Ryan simply shook hands. We piled our things into the jeep and began the drive back to College. We took turns playing songs from our mp3 players and were delighted to see that we had the same taste in music. We pulled up the house that he rented. It was brick with a steep pointed roof. A chimney sat in front of the living room and towered over the home. It had a huge yard and a lot of space surrounding it. A small wire wreath hung on the door and I was surprised to see that he had decorated it. I got out and he held my hand to the front door. And let me in. The front room was so clean and organized. Shoes sat in a row and a bench sat there on flawless orange tile. I took mine off and stepped into the living room. The room was spotless and the white carpet was white, not yellow. A large TV sat over the fire place and pictures of Ryan and Buck hung on the clean walls that looked like they had just been painted. The furniture was from the Victorian era and looked new. He showed me the kitchen that was recently redone. It was also Victorian in style and it was beautifully decorated. The cabinets were brown and the appliances were a light teal shade. The dining room had the same color scheme and was just as spotless as the rest of the house. He led me into the bedroom and it felt so cozy. A handmade quilt laid on the wooden bed and a teddy bear sat in the middle of two fluffy pillows.

"Did we walk into the wrong house?" I asked joking, pointing to the bear.

"Hey! Don't joke about Mr. Snuggles." He said holding the bear. "My mother gave it to me. And so what if I like a clean house?" He said laughing. I laid on the bed and it felt so comfortable.

"Do you want to go out to eat?" He asked. "I know this great Chinese buffet around the corner."

"Sure!" I said standing up, not having realized how hungry I was. It had been hours since we left my moms.

We both walked around the corner and a blonde yelled Ryan's name. She had large breasts, a small frame, and a preppy attitude. I recognized her as Mandy Russ.

"Hey, Grace. Joey this is Grace. Grace this is Joey, my girlfriend." He said kissing my hand.

"Wow. I never thought you'd be one to get a girlfriend Ryan." She said with jealousy. "Do you still have my number?" She asked.

"I don't actually. I'm sorry." He said as we continued walking.

"Well, don't you want it?" She asking running behind us laughing. Ryan shook his head as we walked past her again. She mumbled something under her breath and she walked away. I felt irritated again.

"Ryan, are girls that you've made out with going to be coming up to us constantly?" I asked.

"Joey, I made the mistake of trying to find what I found in you in a lot of girls. I regret that, but I can't change it. If they do, I will be sure to let them know that you're my girlfriend and that I love you." I stopped in my tracks.

"You love me?" I asked surprised.

"Yes Joey. I love you. Do you really think that I would have made love with you if I didn't?" He said kissing me.

"I love you too Ryan." I said kissing him back.

He hugged me tightly and I proceeded to hold his hand. We walked to the restaurant and sat down. The waitress brought us two Cokes as she stared at Ryan. We got our food and made each other try our favorites. We talked until the restaurant began to close. Ryan grabbed my coat and put it over my shoulders as he kissed me. He handed me the number that the waitress had given him and I ripped it up and threw it on the plate. I had never had something that other people had been jealous of. I knew by the faces of the women that walked by us that they were jealous of me just for being on Ryan's muscular arm. I giggled as he sang classic songs on our way home. He opened the door for me and we took a long relaxing steamy shower together. We went into the room and laid down naked. His body was warm against mine.

"What are we going to tell them Ryan?" I suddenly asked.

"Tell who, what?" He asked, confused.

"Everyone, everything." I answered.
"Jojo, who cares? We're in love. That's all that matters. Now lay your head down and rest, please." He said kissing me.

We fell asleep intertwined and I slept deeply next to him. I woke up to a shuttering noise and Ryan over me. The camera in his hands was vintage and rare. I had been looking for the exact same one since I had first gotten into photography. I laughed as he took the photos.
"Where did you find that?" I asked as her handed it to me.
"In an antique store in Cedar City." He said as he gave it to me. "I knew you'd love it. While you were napping off our first experience, I went into the basement and found the photography stuff. I'm just happy I found the right one." I took photos of him and us together before I kissed him romantically. He smiled at me and told me to relax. Within minutes I heard bacon sizzling. He brought in a tray with a big breakfast on it. It had fresh rose petals and three small candles. We ate it together as the radio played old sixties songs quietly.
"I thought maybe today we could walk around and take some photos with your new camera." He said as he got himself dressed.
"I would love to." I said washing off the dishes and the tray.

Ryan and I walked to a river that had tons of spring wildflowers around it. I went to snap a picture on a ladybug on a petal when I realized I was out of film. Ryan pulled a new cartage out and I popped it open to find a whimsical engagement ring. I held it and dropped the cartridge. Ryan was kneeling in front of me with a broad smile. My heart stopped beating as I anticipated what he was going to say. "Joey. I've never felt this before. This rush of excitement and this comfort of knowing that someone like you can love someone like me. I hope you'll accept this ring as a sign that I want you. I need you. I've never felt more whole in my life. I feel like I've found the missing piece of me. Will you please marry me?" My heart stopped and tears fell from my eyes uncontrollably. Every single thing he had said had sounded like my own heart speaking. I had felt the same way about him.

"Yes Ryan! I'll marry you!" In one motion he brought me into his arms and kissed me. He slid the ring onto my finger and kissed me before he let out all of his held breath.

"Thank you Joey." He said. "You've made me so happy." He filled the film and took our first picture together as an engaged couple. The same picture that I was showing to my mom and Buck now.

"I love him mom." I said as she shook her head and Ryan held my hand.

"Joey, I'm torn." She said as she kissed me on the forehead. "If it were any other circumstance, I'd be thrilled."

"Mother. Please." I begged.

"Honey. You could never do anything to make me not love you." She said leaning into me. "I give you my blessing for the wedding."

"And I give you mine." Buck said as he hugged us both. Ryan Kissed me, and I couldn't help but smile as my mom looked at my engagement ring and hugged us.

THE END

The Ride of Her Life
Kathleen Hope

Table of Contents

Chapter 1: A New Start

Chapter 2: Settling In

Chapter 3: Fire

Chapter 4: Hope From The Ashes

Chapter 1: A New Start

June pulled up to the ranch in a Ford Sedan feeling entirely out of place. She hadn't really been around this sort of rural environment since she was a kid, but it was time to get the hell out of the city. So here she was. An old man who could have been her grandfather walked out of the house. "You must be June."

"Yes, sir." She gave him a smile.

"I'm Roger." He eyed the car a moment, then gestured her inside, out of the blazing heat that baked her skin as soon as she stepped out of the air conditioned car.

Squinting as she stepped into the more dimly lit house, June looked around, reminded all the more of her grandparents place and summers as a kid. He led her to the kitchen. "So I understand you know how to work with horses? Got experience, you said. "

"Yes sir. I haven't done it in a long time, but I'm glad for the opportunity to do so again." June brushed her hair back. "I used to spend my summers on my grandparents ranch and my dad had some horses too. Mostly for show though."

"Just decided to get out of the city?" he asked. "Tea?"

"Yes, please. And it was time. I missed being out in the country like this. I appreciate the opportunity you're giving me, sir."

He poured her a glass of iced tea and looked her over. "Finish that and I'll introduce you to my grandson. He's the main one I have working with the horses, but I think it'll help him to have another hand around. Besides, I want to see how you do."

"Of course," she said. "Thank you." She finished it fairly quickly, aware of him watching her and wondering if that had been a test too as she handed the empty glass back and he put it in the sink.

They walked back outside and past a small garden. "If you get the job, there's an old bunkhouse you can stay in," he said, pointing to a ramshackle building next to the barn. She idly wondered if it even met safety codes. "No problem."

He gave a small grunt in response and led her to the corral where a man only a couple years older than herself was walking a horse. "Harlan, this is that girl I was telling you about."

Harlan looked up at her and June was struck by his dark hair and blue eyes. "You're here to work the horses?" he asked, just a hint of condescension to his voice.

"Yep," June smiled, ignoring the tone.

He clucked at the horse and brought it to a stop. "Let's see what you can do," he said. Harlan walked the horse over to the corral and let it loose, before going to the barn and taking out another horse. This one had a bit of a wild look in its eye, mane and coat a dark black, with a crackle of white on its nose. *Good*, thought June, *perfect way to prove I can handle a horse.*

"This one here is Lightning," said Harlan.

"Unbroken, right? Okay." June slipped into the corral and took the lead. Harlan stepped back, but not out. The horse looked her over and started to pull away with a decisive snort. June spoke low and didn't let him walk away. With another soft command she got him to start walking, going slowly in a circle. He pulled away from her a few more times, but she kept him going, not letting him take control away from her.

June was happy to realize this felt like breathing. Or maybe riding a bicycle. She'd been reading up on the subject since she'd decided to find a job and it was paying off now. Suddenly the horse went at her instead of pulling. She gave it a firm command and didn't back away, getting it back to the walking it had been doing. Out of the corner of her eye she saw the two men share a look.

"That's enough, June," said Roger, nodding to Harlan.

Still looking a bit unhappy about the whole situation, Harlan took the horse back from her.

"Come on, June, let's go over the paperwork and get you settled."

"Thank you, sir," she said. "Nice to meet you, Harlan."

He gave her half a nod and focused on the horse. June followed Roger back into the house. "He'll relax," he said. "Sometimes I think Harlan is as skittish as some of our horses. You just keep handling the horses right and he'll come around."

"Thank you." She sat at the table where he gestured too and brought out some paperwork.

June read it over. Everything was like they'd agreed over the phone. The pay wasn't great, but with somewhere to sleep it was making up for some of it. When she finished, she drove her car up to the ramshackle bunk house and stepped inside.

It wasn't quite so awful inside, but it still needed work. At least there was a bathroom and running water. "You can eat with us in the house," said Roger. "Just ain't got an extra bedroom right now."

"It's fine," smiled June. "Least this way I'm close to the horses."

Roger nodded. "I'll let you get settled. You need anything, you come on up to the house, just come in. I'll get you a key too."

"Okay. Thank you again."

June watched him leave, then went to unpack her car. There wasn't much, but she'd been determined to start over here. Smiling to herself, she grabbed her cowboy hat and put it on, checking herself out in the mirror. It was still fairly new, but it would be broken in sooner rather than later.

Humming to herself, June put her few things away and hung up a picture of her father. It was the one thing she'd done in every place she lived, city or country. Smiling, June looked around and headed back outside.

Harlan was still working the paddock. She walked over to watch, leaning on the fence. He had a sure hand, which was always important when dealing with horses. He ignored her presence, keeping his focus only on the horse. June had done her research and she knew that Harlan was one of the best in the area, which was why the other reason why he worked for his grandfather. Hopefully he didn't feel overly threatened by her being here.

After a while, Harlan finished what he was doing, and looked at her now. She was caught by his blue eyes, seeming to peer into her. His brown hair was just a bit on the long side, hanging underneath his hat.

"Suppose I should introduce you to the rest of the herd," he said.

June smiled. "I'd like that."

Harlan nodded and clucked at the horse he was with, walking it towards the corral. He pointed out each horse and gave their name and a little bit about them. June listened closely, not only because it was important to know, but because he had a gravelly voice that kept her attention.

"Then there's more in the barn," he said, leading her that way. "You've got the bunkhouse, yeah?"

"Yep. So I'm close to the barn if there's ever any need in the middle of the night."

"Not too often, but I have to admit I'll be glad for it. I've slept in the loft a time or two." Harlan got the doors and June stepped inside, giving her eyes a chance to adjust.

"Your grandfather has a lot of horses, doesn't he?" she asked as they moved deeper, the smell of hay and horses comforting and familiar.

"Yeah. We've been working this land since at least his grandfather was a boy. We've always been horse people. What about you? He said you've got experience, and I can see that you're rusty, but you've got some." Harlan was looking her over.

June ignored the slight barb. "I grew up on a place like this. Not this big, my father only had a couple horses. But he taught me most of what I know. And what I don't know I learned on my grandparents place. It was more this side, though still not as big."

Harlan nodded and led her down the stalls. He pointed out which horses were new and which ones were pregnant. "We've got a couple pretty good studs in the area, though he doesn't always use them."

I'll be you have some good studs, thought June, then mentally smacked herself for the thought. They were coworkers and more than that, he was the boss's grandson. "Does your father work here?" she asked instead.

Harlan shook his head. "My dad left when I was young. Roger is my mom's grandfather. She lives in town, handles some of the business side of things."

"Oh. Sorry to hear that. My dad raised my pretty much by himself."

Harlan looked at her, maybe with a little more respect in his eyes. "You seem to have done all right for yourself.

"You too."

Harlan cracked a slight smile at her and took her out to meet the foals.

Eventually, they ended up back at the house for supper. She was a bit surprised to realize that Roger had cooked for them, but quickly covered it up. The food was plain, but filling. He smiled at her as she ate. "I'm too old to go chasing stallions," he said with a smile, "and I like to cook. Sometimes anyway. Keeps me busy."

"Well, it's a great place you've got here. I can see how well you take care of your stock."

Roger scooped her another bit of potatoes. "They're good horses and I know I can trust Harlan to take care of them for me. And that's why I hired you. Getting to be just a little more than one person can handle."

"I'll do my best not to let you down, sir."

"No, I am certain that you won't." Roger said, giving her a wide smile.

Chapter 2: Settling In

June got to work in earnest the next day. It was hard work, but she found things were coming back to her quickly, even if she did end up on her ass more than once. Harlan was dealing with his own horses, but she could tell he was keeping an eye on her too. It made June all that more determined to do this job right and well. She noticed he'd given her one that was half-trained already to start with, but that was fine.

In the late afternoon, after lunch, she helped muck out the stables. Nothing like being ankle deep in this to build some comradeship, she supposed. Harlan certainly never complained as he worked and she didn't either, thought part of her wanted to ask how she was doing and if he thought she'd do as well at this as she thought.

After that it was feeding and brushing down and all the other little things that were involved with taking good care of horses. Roger cooked dinner again and when all was said and done for the day, June went back to her bunkhouse and fell asleep reading a book almost as soon as she lay out on her bed.

The next week or so passed in much the same way. She and Harlan didn't speak much, but she hoped she was earning at least a little bit of grudging respect. The horses were coming along beautifully and if she had a few missteps, at least she was allowed to correct them and learn from her mistakes.

On the weekends, Harlan and Roger would take horses to show, leaving June alone on the land to mind the rest of the horses. She was glad for the opportunity to show her ability to be responsible and to make sure everything was as it should be by the time they got back.

It was kind of nice to be alone with the animals. Not that she minded Harlan's presence, or the way that he watched her. The place was fairly quiet and she took one of the horses down some of the trails, getting more of a feel for the property and making sure the horse could handle everything at the same time. It was nice to be out among so much quiet after the business of the city; June hadn't realized just how much she'd missed this.

As the day wore on, June cooked them dinner, finishing just as the men got home. Roger half-joked he should have her do more often when he tasted it. "Could give you a raise for cooking as well as taking care of the horses."

"Thank you sir, but I'd rather stick with the horses," smiled June.

Harlan, as usual, said nothing, but he did clean his plate and for that June was grateful.

A few days later was when trouble really found them. June was just walking a horse back to the corral when she heard a whinny followed by muffled cursing. She hurried her horse inside, then ran back over to Harlan, who was still on the ground, the horse as far away from him as possible in the smaller training pen. Of course it was Lightning. At least he hadn't Harlan or anything.

"You okay?" asked June, approaching cautiously in case Lightning bolted or kicked.

"Nope," grunted Harlan. "Get him back to the barn. I'm going to need help."

June nodded and got the horses lead. He tried to fight her, tossing his head and stomping, but she was having none of it. With a little more wrestling and some firm words, she got Lightning into the barn and into his pen. He kicked at the door after she closed it, but June ignored the pout and hurried back out to Harlan.

He was trying to get up with help from the fence, clearly favoring one leg. "Here, you idiot, let me help you. I was coming right back."

June put his arm around her shoulder and helped the taller man to his feet. They made their way carefully out of the pen and back towards the house. "Lightning threw you?" asked June.

"Yep. I landed wrong. Pretty sure it's just a sprain, but well, need to get it checked." He grit his teeth as they made their way up the stairs.

Roger was doing some work in the living room, but he bolted to his feet as they came in through the kitchen. "Harlan got thrown, thinks it's a sprain," said June.

Coming over, Roger took her place next to him. "I'll take him on into the clinic."

"Do that. I'll make sure everything is taken care of here."

Roger gave her a short nod and murmured something to his grandson as he helped him out to the car. June watched as he carefully climbed into the pickup truck. She walked back out to the corrals and picked up Harlan's hat where it had fallen.

Getting hurt more or less came with the job. She'd had a few sprains and dislocations herself. Still, it was never fun when you were the one on the receiving end of it. She dusted the hat off and brought it inside, setting it on the table and going to see about the rest of the animals.

June remained tense until she heard the sound of the truck coming back up the drive. She finished what she was doing and came back out, watching Harlan get out of the truck with a pair of crutches. He gave her a pained smile. "Yup, it's a sprain."

"Well, I suppose it's good that ya'll hired me then," she said, smiling but concerned.

"I'll be back on my feet in no time." He hesitated. "But I know you'll take care of things."

"Thank you, Harlan," she said honestly. Roger looked between them, then went to get the door for Harlan.

It was a bit more work that night, getting everything cleaned up and all the horses put away. She went back to check on Lightning. He seemed to have calmed down and she carefully went into his pen. "Hey, I know you didn't mean for him to get hurt. You were scared and you don't like some of this stuff. But we'll take care of you." She patted him and stepped back out, only to see Harlan watching her from the door of the barn. "Aren't you supposed to have your foot up with ice?"

"Is he okay?" Harlan asked instead.

"Yeah. I'll take him out and work him some more tomorrow. Just stubborn."

Harlan nodded. "I've a few that are pretty stubborn in my time. Come on up to the house, dinner's ready."

June smiled at him. "Okay."

They took a few more steps in silence until Harlan spoke again. "Thank you."

"You're welcome. I'm just glad you weren't hurt worse."

"Me too. And you handled Lightning well too." Harlan gave her a smile.

"He kicked the door when I put him away," she admitted. "Stubborn, like I said."

"You'll get him, I'm sure of it. And I'll be back in the saddle as soon as I can."

"I have no doubt of it."

They reached the house and June got the door for him. Roger winked at the pair as they came in. "Ignore anything Harlan tells you, he's hopped up on pain meds."

"I am not," grumbled Harlan, sitting at the table.

"I think he just wanted to get out of doing the dishes," smiled June, moving to help put dinner out.

"Could be, could be. There are stories I have about when he was little…"

Harlan groaned. "Please, Grandpa."

Roger chuckled and patted his arm. They all settled in to eat. June realized that even with Harlan's injury she felt comfortable here. At home. Of course, now she had twice as much work to do by herself, but no doubt Harlan would be back on his feet sooner rather than later.

Chapter 3

They found a new routine over the next day. June worked her horse, taking special care to work on Lightning. He still seemed a bit skittish, but he seemed calmer with her. Roger came out to help with feeding and mucking the barn. "Never let it be said that I refused to muck a barn just because I'm old enough to be retired. I'm pretty sure I'll still be mucking the barn the day before I kick off."

June chuckled. "I'm pretty sure mucking the barn was the first and last chore my Dad ever did too."

"When did you lose him?" Roger asked.

"Late last year. That's when I knew I wanted to get out of the city and back to this. He owed to much on the land for me to keep it after he went, but I think it's okay. Hadn't been in our family that long, not like this. It was just always his dream to raise horses. So I suppose part of me feels like I'm doing this for him."

"As long as you enjoy it too. Can't go living someone else's dream." Roger watched her closely.

"I'm not. I love this. Well, maybe not mucking, but I love working with the horses and watching them grow and develop.

I love knowing that I'm part of what makes them better or more useful or more tame."

"And that right there is why I hired you," said Roger. "I'm glad you and Harlan are getting along too."

"Yeah, we are. He's a good man."

"I know, and I'm glad you were there when he got hurt. He'll be right as rain soon enough."

Chapter 3: Fire

After the first couple of days, Harlan came out to watch her work. Evidently he couldn't stand being cooped up in the house longer than necessary. June could understand that completely. At least he didn't second guess while she worked, letting her do what she needed to do.

Lightning was getting better too. The third day after Harlan started coming out, Lightning went over to him. June watched as Harlan patted his snout and whispered to him. She felt a warmth in her heart as she watched him. Then she firmly reminded herself, again, that they were coworkers and she hadn't come out on this job just to snag a cowboy of her own.

Still, the way Harlan watched her seemed to have changed too. He smiled a little more when he talked to her, maybe sat a little closer at dinner. She stayed longer in the house afterward too, just talking or watching television with him. Roger said nothing, but she could tell he was pleased.

About a week and a half later, Roger announced that he had to go out of town for a few days to deal with some business. "I know you two can more than handle the place, he told them," watching them closely. "Harlan you're in charge, but don't do anything too crazy."

"I won't," he promised. "Besides, I'm still a gimp."

"You'll be fine. I know the place will be in good hands. I'm leaving tomorrow morning, early."

"We'll take care of everything," promised June.

He did leave as planned. Harlan came out to watch her work as usual. Lightning seemed a little nervous as she put him back in the barn, but he followed her commands.

They went back to the house for dinner. Harlan had fixed something simple and they sat together at the table, without Roger.

June pushed her food around a bit. "I'm glad you're getting better."

"I should be off crutches next week," Harlan said. "At this rate I'm working to help you rather than the other way around."

June chuckled. "I just want you to be well enough to push around a broom in the barn."

"Ah yes, mucking is everyone's favorite job," smiled Harlan. June caught his blue eyes and they shared a gaze for a long moment before she looked away.

"You better put that ankle up for a while. I'll do the dishes," said June, standing and gathering them up.

Harlan continued to watch her. "Come hang out for a while when you're done. Maybe we can watch a movie or something."

"Okay." June smiled at him and went to clean up. She took a few deep breaths as she ran the hot water and soap. Maybe Harlan was starting to look at her a little differently too. Well she could either dance around the issue or she could do something about it.

Mind made up, she finished the dishes and went out to the living room. Harlan was on the sofa, flipping through channels. June sat next to him. As his eyes were focused on the television, she reached over and put her hand over his.

Harlan raised an eyebrow then took her hand as he picked out something to watch. He didn't speak about it, and neither did she, but they held hands for the rest of the evening, relaxing and enjoying the movie. When it finished, Harlan squeezed her hand. "I had a good time," he said.

She smiled warmly at him. "Next time I'll pick the movie though. Something with more action."

Harlan laughed. "All right, sounds fair. Have a good night, June."

"You too." June smiled at him a moment longer, then turned and trekked back to the bunkhouse. The night was warm and she pushed open a window. Maybe she might be able to tame more than horses here. She laughed at her own cheesiness and started getting ready for bed.

Suddenly, a loud whinny caught her attention. Frowning, she pulled her boots back on and headed for the barn. Something felt wrong and as she neared the doors she thought she smelled smoke. Biting back panic, she flung the doors open. Now there was more noise and though she couldn't see flames that didn't mean there wasn't fire.

"Harlan!" she yelled at the house, though she had no idea if he could hear her. There wasn't time anyway as she darted into the barn and started opening up the doors. The smoke was definitely getting thicker and she covered her mouth as she tried to lead panicking horses to safety.

She could hear Harlan's voice as she reached the last few. Lightning ducked his head as she opened his pen last and she took the hint, swinging up on his back and riding out on him, just as the barn burst into real flames, loft cracking ominously above her.

"June!" Harlan pulled her down, hugging her tightly. Lightning whinnied at them. June reached over and pet the horse, then led him over to the corral where Harlan had put the others.

"I'm okay," she told Harlan, turning to look at the barn.

"Thank goodness." He put an arm around her and held her close. "I saw the smoke and called the fire department."

"Probably be too late for the barn. I'm sorry."

Harlan shook his head. "The horses are okay and so are you. That's what's really important. Insurance can cover the other things."

There was the sound of sirens approaching and the herd nervously galloped to the far end of the corral. "You shouldn't be standing on that foot and there isn't much we can do out here," she said as the fire truck pulled up.

"You get the horses out okay, Harlan?" asked a man maybe a couple years older than him.

"June did. I gotta call Grandpa." He started limping towards the house, evidently leaving his crutches behind in his hurry.

June put her arm around him again and helped him into the house. "Do you want me to stay with you or see to the horses?"

Harlan rubbed his face. "Better see to the horses, I guess." He took a breath and picked up the phone. June went to the kitchen door but stayed for the moment to make sure he was okay. "Grandpa we have a problem," he said, rubbing his temples. "Barn caught fire. The horses are fine, but I think we've lost everything else."

June glanced to make sure the horses were still in their corral, then walked back and squeezed Harlan's hand as he listened to the other end of the line.

"I understand. Drive safe, Grandpa. The barn's already gone; you getting in a wreck hurrying home won't bring it back."

Harlan sighed and looked up at June. Impulsively, she leaned down and kissed his forehead. "We'll get through this."

He smiled sadly at her. "I'm glad you're here."

"Me too. Lightning helped out too you know."

"Well, he's a smart horse, just stubborn."

June met his gaze and knew they weren't just talking about the horse any more.

Chapter 4: Hope From The Ashes

Roger got in a few hours later after the fire department had done all that they could. June and Harlan had fallen asleep together on the sofa, leaning against one another. "Well good morning, kids," he said as he walked in the front door, startling them awake.

He walked through the house and opened up the back door to look at the wreck of the barn. At least the bunk house was fairly undamaged and the horses seemed to be okay in the corral. He turned back to the other two. "I bought some hay. Let's make sure they're fed and then we can go over the damage.

The rest of the day Roger and Harlan spent going over the insurance figuring out was salvageable and what wasn't. June spent most of her time with the horses and the vet who was making sure they were actually all okay. There was some smoke inhalation, but they seemed to be fine for the most part, if a bit annoyed that there wasn't a barn to take shelter in when it started to rain.

Roger came out to see her after a while. "Harlan told me what you did. I wanted to thank you."

June gave a smile. "Just part of the job, sir."

"Still, that was very brave of you. Have to see what the insurance will cover, but if I can, I'm giving you a bonus."

"That's not why I did it," said June.

"I know. And that's why you deserve it. I'm going into town to take care of a few things. I'll be back later on tonight." He turned and headed for his truck.

Harlan made his way out as he left. "You doing okay?"

June yawned. "Yeah, I think so. He wants to give me a bonus."

"I know. I hope he can." He led June towards the bunkhouse. "Come on, I know you didn't hardly sleep last night."

"You didn't either," protested June, tugging him inside with her.

Harlan lost his balance and stumbled forward, knocking her into the bed. "Oh God, I'm…"

He was cut off by June planting one big kiss on him. He groaned into it and buried a hand in her hair, knocking her hat to the floor.

They kissed like that for a long time, exploring one another's mouths. He tasted fresh and his lips were surprisingly soft. June's hands stroked down his back, feeling the broad muscles under his shirt. She moaned against him and he slid a thigh between her legs. June rocked up against him as they continued to kiss.

Finally, Harlan pulled back. "Do you want to?" he asked.

"God yes," muttered June. "There's lube and condoms in the bag in the bathroom. Didn't see a point in throwing those away when I came out here."

"I'm glad you didn't," he smiled, limping over to fetch the bag.

June groaned. "I should have got that for you."

"I'm not helpless," smiled Harlan, coming back and kissing her again. He reached to unbutton her shirt, still tasting her lips. His hands were rough on her skin as he pushed June's shirt off.

June smiled at him and reached back to undo her bra. "Still, we don't need you on crutches for an extra three weeks because you pushed yourself. Come here." She guided him to lay on his back, undoing his shirt in return as he reached up to fondle her breasts, running his thumbs over her nipples.

Stepping back, June undid her jeans and pushed her pants and underwear down, leaving herself naked. Harlan clearly appreciated the view. "Anybody tell you you're beautiful?" he asked.

"Not lately." She stepped out of her boots and the pooled clothing and climbed back into bed, straddling his chest as she opened his jeans.

Harlan kissed her thigh and started touching her, making her moan softly as she freed his cock, kissing the head of it before licking the shaft. He held her hip and pulled her down so he could start to tongue the softer folds of skin, using his fingers as well.

June moaned softly and went down on him, enjoying the spikes of pleasure he was sending down her spine. He groaned against her as they pleasured one another until finally she pulled away and turned around, grabbing a condom.

Harlan pulled her down for another kiss as she rolled it on and prepared him. She kept kissing him as he guided her inside, both of them moaning in unison as she started to move.

The bunkhouse was quiet except for the sounds of them moving together. Everything still smelled faintly of smoke and burning hay, but she could easily ignore it as her full attention was focused on Harlan. He reached up to toy with her breasts again as she rode him slowly, taking her time.

Finally she could tell by his breathing that he was getting close. She shifted herself and he grabbed her hips, fucking her harder, making her gasp until she came just a few moments before he did.

Panting, she lay across his chest and kissed him again slowly as he moved for just a few moments longer.

When he finally ceased, she carefully pulled off and binned the condom. Harlan reached for her and June curled up against his side.

"We ought to get dressed before Grandpa gets back," he muttered.

"We got time," smiled June. "Are you in a hurry?"

"No, not at all." Harlan pulled her close and they fell asleep, just like that.

THE END

Dominated In Every Position
Kathleen Hope

Table of Contents

Chapter 1: Uncharted Territory

Chapter 2: Meeting Temptation

Chapter 3: Unleashing Desire

Chapter 4: Unbridled Instinct

Chapter 1: Uncharted Territory

"Camping is definitely not my thing," Emma thought dryly to herself as she surveyed her work.

The dilapidated tent in front of her was testament to her incompatibility with the great outdoors. She had been certain she could manage a few metal poles and some canvas fabric—she was a doctor for flip's sake—but an hour after removing the tent's components from their neat and tidy carrying bag and battling with which pole went where, she realized that pitching a tent required a skill-set that she simply did not possess.

She should have known that this was not a good fit for her when her brother, Adam, and his girlfriend showed up to fetch her this morning. They couldn't contain their laughter as she walked out of the house wearing a pair of Marciano capris and Diane von Furstenberg wrap top on her curvaceous figure, toting her favorite Louis Vuitton rolling luggage.

"You do realize we're not camping at the Hilton, right sis?" her brother had teased.

"Very funny," she retorted, as she picked up the too-heavy suitcase and dropped it in his trunk.

It hadn't crossed her mind that there would be no electrical outlet available for her blow-dryer or curling iron, and she certainly couldn't have imagined a vacation destination where she wouldn't have access to a decent size mirror. She might have lightened her makeup case if she had realized she'd be applying it using nothing more than her compact mirror as a guide. Then again, if she had been made aware of the lack of amenities on this trip, she wouldn't have lightened anything; she would have gone to the Hilton instead.

She took a deep breath and exhaled heavily, trying to blow away the frustration she felt for the canvas monstrosity. She knew her brother had finished pitching his tent ages ago, so had no doubt that the eyes she felt boring into the back of her head were his, mocking her silently.

"OK, I give. How the heck do you put this thing together?" Emma conceded.

"I'll help. We'll have it together in no time," Julie, Adam's girlfriend, piped up before he could lay in with more jests at his sister's expense.

While Julie was a city girl, just like Emma, she had apparently spent more time in the wilderness because it only took her about five minutes to fix Emma's tent-constructing mishap. Or perhaps she took a crash course in camping 101 to avoid Adam's mocking humor.

Adam sauntered over to where the women stood admiring Julie's handiwork.

"Now that wasn't so bad, was it, Em?" he queried good-naturedly.

"You know, when you said we were headed to an upscale campground for the weekend, I was thinking cottages with indoor plumbing and satellite TV, not a tent and a cooler of staples," Emma observed drolly.

"Ahhh. How else was I going to convince you to come along?" he teased.

"In all seriousness though, Em, it's been ages since we spent any time together, and I thought if we could get out of 'on-call' range, we could at least have a whole weekend together," he admitted.

How was Emma supposed to be mad at him now? She had no idea that Adam had been missing their time together. She just figured that he'd been as busy with his life as she'd been with hers. Suddenly, her frustration seemed to vanish, and Emma was glad to be with her brother again, even if it meant having to spend a whole weekend in the middle of nowhere. Someplace even her cell phone range didn't dare venture apparently, she realized as she checked her phone out of habit.

Dropping her phone back into her purse, Emma wandered over to her brother's SUV. After a three hour drive to the remote campsite and an hour and a half trying to pitch a tent, she was famished. However, after opening the lid to the cooler, she realized that the hot dogs inside were not currently in an edible condition.

"Oh, great," she thought.

"I don't suppose this campsite comes equipped with an electric oven?" she called playfully to her brother.

Adam rolled his eyes and looked to find the site's fire pit.

"Tell you what. Julie and I will go round up some sticks and wood for a fire, and you just hang out and take it easy for a few minutes," he proposed.

"Besides, I could use a little…alone time…with my girlfriend if you know what I mean." Adam winked at Emma to emphasize his meaning, grasped Julie's hand in his own and the two headed off beyond the clearing and into the trees beyond.

Chapter 2: Meeting Temptation

Emma couldn't remember the last time she had absolutely nothing she had to do. It was such a foreign feeling that within minutes she felt like she was going stir crazy. Her life didn't usually provide opportunity for leisure; she was a third-year resident surgeon at NewYork-Presbyterian hospital in Manhattan, and what little time she didn't spend at the hospital, she spent engaged in a charity outreach program with the hospital. She had been longing for more down-time lately, but now that she found herself with nothing to do, she realized that she didn't care for it much.

She looked around for something to keep her preoccupied--a distraction from her inactivity—and found it in the trunk of Adam's vehicle. She popped the trunk, heaved her luggage out and rolled it over to her tent. She could at least get herself settled while her brother and his girlfriend were out having a little fun, since this was going to be her makeshift home for the next two days. After struggling to get her luggage inside the tent, she returned to the car for the extra blankets and pillows Adam had tossed on the backseat, knowing Emma wouldn't know to pack these essentials.

As she turned to make her way back to her tent, a noise in the distance caught her attention. At first, she assumed the sound of crunching leaves and twigs must have been Adam and Julie returning to camp. But when she didn't see them appear in the clearing, she was instantly apprehensive. She strained to listen, to determine the precise location of the sound, but her "find-people-in-the-wilderness" skills must have been lacking. She could locate the general direction, but no matter how she tried, she could not find the source. It was clear by now that the sounds were indeed some sort of footsteps, but the gait did not sound human. And that thought scared her even more.

Emma had no idea what sort of wildlife occupied this wooded area. Wolves? Coyote? Bears? Big Foot!?! As the noise got closer, her mind conjured images of every wilderness-based horror movie she'd ever seen and she began to long for the safety of her cozy Manhattan apartment. And then she saw something. In fact, she saw two somethings. She couldn't decipher exactly what they were, shrouded by the trees and brush of the forest, but whatever the figures were, they were huge. And, for a brief second, she saw the eyes of one of the figures. They stared at her, and then just as quickly as she had seen the two figures watching her in the distance, they were gone.

Emma was so shaken by the experience that she locked herself in Adam's car and waited for his return. And then she worried for her brother. What if the huge creatures found her brother and Julie? She couldn't just sit there useless, waiting to see if they did in fact return. As scared as she was, it just wasn't in Emma to stay there, safe in the car, while some horrible harm could come to someone she loved.

She unlocked the car and shoved herself out without another thought. She was on her feet and running in the direction she had seen Adam and Julie head earlier. Unfortunately, it was also the direction she had last seen the enormous creatures. She couldn't have run for more than two minutes when she stopped abruptly. Off to one side, she heard the sound of footsteps. She listened for a moment longer and was certain that this time, the steps were made by human feet. Hopefully, Adam and Julie had strayed off their path, and it was them not more than 10 meters away. It was difficult to see through the brush all around her, but she squinted hard and could make out a tall, muscular figure. It was moving slowly forward, toward her, but she couldn't see another figure nearby. Where was Julie? And since when was Adam so tall?

And then she saw him. A tall, muscular, shirtless figure approaching warily. He looked powerful, but somehow the non-threatening way in which he moved told her he was not a danger to her. She stayed frozen in place as the stranger crossed the final few meters between them, and then he was standing directly in front of her. He didn't speak at first; he stared at her for a moment, perhaps assessing whether she posed any threat—though for the life of her she couldn't imagine how she could possibly be a threat to this stranger. It's true that she was tall for a girl, at 5-foot, 9 inches, she could have been a model, if it weren't for the slightly curvier figure than one might see strolling down the fashion runways of Paris. But, Emma never lacked for male attention; her ample breast size was the envy of many a woman. But somehow Emma couldn't fathom how her height or her breast size could appear threatening to this beast of a man. The thought almost made her chuckle aloud, and if it hadn't been for her frayed nerves, she just might have succumbed to laughter.

"Hello. I'm Michael" he said softly, nearly making Emma jump.

"Hi there. Um, you haven't happened to see a tall guy and an attractive woman walking this way, have you?"

Regardless of how tantalizing the figure before her was, she had been in the middle of urgently seeking out her brother, and didn't have time to chat—even if arousal was suddenly coursing through her body and settling between her legs in response to the gorgeous man before her.

"You're the only attractive woman I've seen. And I don't see any man with you," he observed.

Emma blushed just a little, but forced her mind to remain on topic.

"My brother went off with his girlfriend and they haven't returned yet, and I saw some sort of huge animals somewhere this way," Emma went on, her voice sounding more panicked at she continued.

"There is nothing to fear in these woods. I'm sure you don't have to worry about your brother," he replied emphatically.

"Oh, no. I saw something. I'm certain of it," she said looking upward into the strangers eyes.

And then she was silent once again. Those eyes. She knew it wasn't possible, but those were the same eyes she saw staring at her at the camp. While she couldn't possibly describe the rest of the creature, she was able to see those eyes clearly, and she was staring into those same eyes at this very moment. Emma was so confused and as she stood there silent, with recognition radiating from her own eyes, the stranger became perceptibly uncomfortable, almost agitated. A footstep a few meters behind him caught his attention and he was turning around, heading back the way he'd come before Emma could gather her thoughts.

When the sounds of the receding footsteps vanished, Emma shook her head, trying to clear it and remember why she was there. And when thoughts of her brother flashed through her mind, she was on the move once again. She would have to think about the mysterious stranger in the woods later.

Less than a minute later, she thought she heard a noise behind her. She turned her head, not slowing her step, and when she turned back, she ran straight into Adam. She nearly knocked him over, she had been moving with such force, but he maintained his balance and caught Emma before she could fall face first into the ground.

"Going for an afternoon jog, Emma?" he queried with a grin.

"Oh God, no. I saw something. And then they were gone, and I was so worried."

She was still feeling panic course through her, but relief was beginning to spread as the realization that Adam and Julie were OK sunk in.

"Oh, thank goodness you're alright," she panted.

"You saw something? Like what? Bigfoot? I've been to this campground dozens of times, Em, and I've never run into something so much as a stray dog. There is absolutely nothing and no one here. I think your mind must be playing tricks on you," he tried to explain gently.

"But, that's not true. I ran into someone just a minute back there," she pointed in the direction from which she'd come.

"OK, Em. Now you're scaring me. Are you OK? Is this your way of trying to scare me into taking you home? 'Cause if that's what you really want, just say so," Adam responded somewhat sadly.

"No, of course not," she replied emphatically.

And then she realized that she had to stop. Adam didn't believe her, and the more she tried to convince him, the more he would think she was trying to get out of spending time with him this weekend.

She plastered a smile on her face, "Gottcha!" she yelled, trying to convince him now that she had been joking.

"Oh! Good one, Em!"

It must have worked, because Adam beamed at her with a giant smile, thrilled that she was might have been warming up to his good-hearted jokester personality. The three walked back to the campsite together, Emma certain she could hear faint sounds in the distance resembling the unhuman gait she had heard earlier. But she remained silent.

Chapter 3: Unleashing Desire

The day progressed without any further upsets. Adam got a fire going shortly after they returned and the group roasted hot dogs for dinner and then marshmallows later on as they sat around the fire, sharing childhood memories with Julie. Some were heartwarming and others made even Adam blush a little. Emma was enjoying herself so much that she forgot about the unsettling events of the afternoon. That was, until she crawled into her tent, tired and ready for sleep. And then she was wide awake, and her nerves made her painfully attuned to every noise in the forest. She laid there for hours, listening to crickets, small rodents and birds playing beneath the blanket of stars. Every noise made her jump and quake in fear. It was the early hours of the morning before Emma finally drifted off into a restless slumber. And she could never have anticipated what would happen when she awoke the following day.

The sun was barely breaking through the dark of the night's sky when her eyes fluttered open. Some noise must have brought her to a state of semi-consciousness, but she couldn't remember what noise it was. She had rolled during her sleep and now laid pressed up against one side of the tent. She rolled to try to center her position within the tent, but found her movement blocked by something solid behind her. And suddenly she was wide awake. Her eyes flew open and her mouth opened to scream. A hand came up quickly to cover her lips.

"Shhhhh," a voice said soothingly.

The tall, muscular man she had run into yesterday laid shirtless, propped up on an elbow beside her.

"I promise I don't mean you any harm. I had to see you again. I don't know what it is about you, Emma, but I could not stop thinking of you after I saw you standing in the clearing yesterday," the stranger tried to explain.

But, he had given away too much already. Emma's mind immediately returned to yesterday's events. She wasn't standing in a clearing when she ran into this man, but she was when she first saw those eyes. Emma had no idea what to make of that, and right now it wasn't the first priority in her mind.

"I could not stay away Emma," he continued, and it was the absolute truth.

Michael had no idea what had compelled him to watch her in the clearing, nor did he know why he purposely found her later in the woods as she searched for her brother. And he could not fathom what had compelled him here now. He was attracted to her in a way he had never been attracted to another woman. His brother had felt the same compulsion toward her, but must have possessed more strength than Michael because he was able to stay away.

"Please do not scream," Michael continued pleadingly as he moved his hand away from her mouth.

"How do you know my name?" she queried, remaining absolutely still.

She was certain that she would be no physical match for this man so all she could do was talk.

"I overheard your brother speaking to you after you were reunited yesterday," he admitted honestly.

"Your eyes...." Emma began.

She wasn't able to form a coherent sentence, but she had to voice what she was thinking. Something about this man terrified her but also stirred something she couldn't quite decipher. She wanted to scream and run, while at the same time, she wanted to throw herself at him.

"What about my eyes Emma?" he queried ever so softly.

"I've seen them before...before we met yesterday. I know I have, and yet that's not possible...is it?" she asked, unsure of anything at that moment.

Michael didn't know what compelled him to admit the truth to this woman he barely knew—had only spoken to for a brief moment.

"It is possible, Emma."

"But...you're human, and what I saw was definitely not." She was now far more puzzled than terrified.

"I am human, Emma. But I am also not," he confessed mysteriously.

She continued to stare into his eyes, mesmerized; thoroughly captivated by this enigma before her. And then, ever so slowly, his head moved downward toward hers. He gave her plenty of time to resist, to push him away or demand that he stop. But she continued to gaze into his eyes, and then his lips pressed gently against hers, staying still for a moment and then pressing harder, his tongue gliding along her lips. And when her lips began to move against his, his tongue gently began to ply her lips open, silently requesting entry into the warmth of her mouth. She granted him access immediately, and her tongue came out to meet his.

Emma had no idea what had come over her. This man, if indeed he was a man, who had terrified her only moments before was suddenly the object of her desire. She craved his hands on her body; his tongue on her skin and his cock deep inside her. It was innate, purely an animal drive deep inside her that was responding to the primitive need radiating from Michael's body.

His hand came up to her jaw and slowly began trailing down the length of her neck, past her collarbone to cup one of her big tits in his hand. He squeezed gently and rubbed a finger back and forth across her nipple. Emma moaned against his mouth and deepened the kiss as he hands came up to the back of his neck. He squeezed harder and then slid his hand between them to cup her other tit and squeeze her nipple gently. He wanted to touch every part of her; leave no inch without the scent of his own skin.

Emma's hand glided down Michael's back and as her fingers grazed along his skin he let out a guttural moan that sounded fierce, and she knew without a doubt that Michael was more than just an ordinary man. The knowledge sent a fiery heat coursing through her, making her pussy throb. His hand continued exploring Emma's body, skimming over her soft belly and hips. When his hand teased her by gently grazing her clit, she moaned in response, not recognizing the sound of her own voice.

"Oh, God Emma. I want every part of you," he whispered huskily, and she moaned against his lips in response.

He was overwhelmed with lust, desperate to fuck her, but not wanting this to be over too soon. He kissed her mouth one more time and then began to press his lips against her chin, her neck. When he reached the top of her shirt his hands came up and tore it in one swift tug, baring her gorgeous tits to his view.

He moved back to look at her for a moment and then returned his lips to her body, kissing along the upper swells of her tits, crossing back and forth from one to the other and then sucking a nipple in his mouth. As he released her nipple from his mouth and trailed to the other, he bit down ever so gently on her nipple, nibbling just enough to make Emma moan loudly in pleasure. His lips then followed the path his hands had taken only moments before, kissing, licking and nipping at the soft flesh of her stomach.

When her capris interfered with his tongue's path, his hands came up once again and tore them open. He pulled them off her body quickly and then returned his lips to the smooth, shaved mound above her pussy. He let his tongue slide briefly over her clit before moving onto her fleshy thighs and she writhed beneath him, trying to press her clit against his lips again. He breathed deeply, the intoxicating scent of her pussy making him dizzy with arousal. It made him want to shove his rock hard cock deep inside her. But instead, he slid two fingers along her slit and spread her lips open. He stared at her pussy for a moment and then all of a sudden delved deep with his tongue, plunging in and out, mimicking the movements his cock longed for. Emma dug her fingers into Michael's shoulders, writhing wildly beneath his tongue.

"Oh God Michael!" she cried out.

"Yes Emma, that's it. Cum for me now," he instructed.

And her body was more than happy to oblige. As Michael's tongue penetrated her pussy one more time, she began to spasm around his tongue, bucking wildly and forcing his tongue deeper.

And Michael could wait no longer. In one swift movement, his jeans were off and he was on top of Emma, poised at her entrance. She closed her eyes, anticipating the feeling of his massive cock filling her sopping wet pussy. He pressed forward gently, penetrating her slowly and when he had slid every inch of his cock inside her, he remained still, giving her a moment to adjust to his size.

And then he began to move, thrusting his cock deep into her pussy, withdrawing slowly until just the tip of his cock remained inside, and then plunging back in. Emma opened her eyes. Her position provided her with an unobstructed view of the outside through the opening of her tent.

What she saw there should have terrified her but she was too engrossed in pleasure to feel fear. There in front of her was a massive, jet black, fierce-looking bear standing on its hind legs. Her gaze traveled from its massive hind legs along the length of its body covered in shimmering fur and to his eyes. Emma gasped aloud. Though the eyes she saw were not Michael's eyes, they were so similar. In that moment, she was certain this is what Michael had meant when he said he was both human and not.

This is what Michael would look like in his alternate form—a massive, powerful animal. And the thought sent a fiery arousal through her body unlike anything she had ever experienced before. It was enough to send her over the edge, and she began to cum, screaming her pleasure as Michael thrust deep inside her pussy and the gorgeous, furred beast, who she was certain could take human form, watched every second.

Chapter 4: Unbridled Instinct

As the aftershocks of orgasm continued to send ripples of pleasure through her body, Michael stilled his movements, remaining above her for just a moment. He knew what was about to happen, and he didn't want Emma running scared when it did.

And right before her eyes, the enormous beast outside began to transform, the fur-covered body morphing slowly into a man covered in sinewy muscle. He was nearly as attractive as Michael, but something about Michael's gentleness came through in his appearance and made him somehow sexier.

The unclothed man outside began to move forward, approaching the tent and then bending down to enter the confines of the canvas structure. Emma experienced a moment of panic, but as she tried to move away from the approaching man, Michael began to move within her once again, distracting her from her emotions, leaving her mind too full of pleasure for anything else.

"This is Gabriel, Emma," Michael leaned down to whisper in her ear.

"He felt the same pull to you that I did yesterday, and I suppose he was unable to resist you either. He should be a part of this, Emma," Michael explained, though the last part he phrased as a question more than a demand.

She nodded almost imperceptibly. But Gabriel's hands were already on Emma's body, squeezing her tits, caressing her neck.

Michael withdrew his cock from her pussy and moved to kneel next to her, opposite Gabriel. Both men covered her body with their hands, caressing her from her ankles to her neck, and every part of her they could access in between. Michael squeezed Emma's tits in his hands, using more force than he had originally anticipated, and Gabriel leaned down to lick her nipples, then suck them into his mouth hard. Emma gasped and arched her back in unexpected pleasure, and the men realized that Emma was so horny her body was beginning to respond uncontrollably to the rough play.

Gabriel slid a hand down Emma's ribs, over her hips and to her cunt. Without warning, he shoved two of his fingers into her pussy and began thrusting them in and out fast, pounding her cunt as hard as he could with his fingers.

She screamed, writhing beneath the men as Michael joined Gabriel in Emma's pussy with his own two fingers, stretching her and hitting a pleasure zone no one had ever managed to stimulate before.

Pressure built up inside her—this feeling was absolutely foreign—and she resisted the sudden urge to pull away from the pressure. Their fingers felt too good, pressing hard against her G-spot, and in the next moment, she experienced an orgasm unlike anything she had ever known. God, she had no idea her pussy could feel that good! She was soaking wet—everything was soaking wet, and she felt like she had died and gone to heaven.

Gabriel laid down on the tent floor beside Emma, and Michael helped her up. When she was on her knees, he guided her toward Gabriel's cock and pressed her down gently at the small of her back. He returned his fingers to her pussy, sliding slowly in and out this time, as Emma opened her mouth wide and took the head of Gabriel's cock in her mouth.

She didn't stop there. She continued to slide as much of his cock into her mouth as she could manage, and then he thrust his hips upward, forcing his cock even further, to the back of Emma's throat. She withdrew nearly all of his cock from her mouth, licking the tip with her tongue and as she was about to sheath his cock with her mouth once again, Michael gently placed one hand on the back of her head and guided her head down, forcing Gabriel's cock to the back of her throat. Michael guided her movements, forcing her just a little further with every thrust until her throat was spasming around Gabriel's cock, making him desperate to cum deep in her throat. But he resisted the urge, and reached down beneath Emma's arms to pull her upward on top of him.

She was poised above his cock. Michael placed his hands on her shoulders and pressed down, forcing Gabriel's cock into her pussy. She moaned loudly and arched her back as she began to ride, one hand coming up to squeeze her own tits as the other moved to her clit and began to rub.

Michael disappeared from her view for a moment, and then he was placing a hand against the small of her back once again. He pressed gently to lean her forward until he lips were poised just above Gabriel's, and then Michael closed the gap by pressing just a little more. Emma's mouth came down on his, and his tongue plunged deep in her mouth, mimicking the thrust of his cock.

She was once again wild with pleasure, so much so that she almost didn't notice Michael, pressing against her ass hole with his wet finger. Emma stopped moving, and she tried to move forward to get away from Michael's finger, but Gabriel's hands caught her around the waist and held her still. But no one had ever touched her there before.

Understanding dawned on Michael instantly, and it made him heady with pleasure, so much so that he could feel himself nearly ready to cum just thinking about being Emma's first.

"I have to experience every part of you, Emma. Please. I promise you will enjoy it, but I have to have you this way."

A split second before she nodded in agreement, Michael's cock replaced his finger, and he was pushing forward gently, giving Emma's body a chance to relax.

And then the head of his cock slipped inside her ass.

"Oh, God, Emma. Your ass feels so good," he groaned.

Slowly, he pushed onward, sliding in the length of his cock until her ass had accepted every inch of him. Again, he remained still, giving her a moment to adjust. Then he could wait no more. He began to thrust forward, gently at first and then with increasing speed and vigor. Gabriel continued to pound Emma's pussy with his cock, and the combination of his cock in her cunt and Michael's dick deep in her ass made her cum hard. The spasms of her orgasm rocked both men. Gabriel was the first to cum, thrusting deep in her pussy. Michael joined him just a moment later, cumming hard and spilling his load deep in Emma's ass.

The three of them were exhausted and collapsed on the floor of the tent, falling asleep almost instantly. It was quite a scene for Adam and Julie to find when they checked on Emma after returning from a long morning stroll through the forest.

THE END

Flames of Passion
Kathleen Hope

Table of Contents

Chapter 1: Troubled Beginnings

Chapter 2: A Change of Heart

Chapter 3: The Perfect Ending

Chapter 1: Troubled Beginnings

Amelie tapped her red Prada pump against the Coffee Shops black tile. Her long beautiful legs were crossed and a cloth napkin laid delicately on her thick thighs. She rolled her pretty blue eyes as the clock past another minute after the time Mona said her blind date would be there. An annoyed sigh escaped her beautiful thick blood red pouting lips, and she twirled her long blonde hair as a woman came through the coffee shop door. Amelie looked out the window and decided to leave. The next person to come through the door was a shorter man with a muscular build. He had fire red curly hair and a baby face that was covered in freckles. Scars from burns also plagued his face. Amelie cringed as he sat down at her table.

"Hello, my name's Parker Moore. You must be Amelie Rose. Mona told me all about you, but her words couldn't do your beauty justice." He said extending his hand, it was also burned and hard for Amelie too look at. Amelie scoffed back and denied his extended over work worn, permanently stained and callused hand. She knew he was the firefighter Mona had told her about. Some friend she was. Mona knew that this man wasn't the kind Amelie was interested in. He last three boyfriends owned islands and paid for them with modeling jobs.

"Ugh, yeah. I think Mona was mistaken though, I'm afraid I'm going to have to cancel the date." Amelie said as she stood up and straightened her designer black dress.

"If this is because I was late I'm so sorry. I got called into work, it was an emergency. I got here as soon as I could. I really would like to apologize properly if you'd allow me too." Parker stumbled on his words, extending his gnarled hand again. The fear of rejection hung in his bright emerald eyes, but he smiled.

"I'm sorry. It's not your timing." Amelie said as she left the coffee house without taking another look at the unattractive man. Amelie watched through the window as Parker sat himself down at the table and held his heavy head in his arms.

Amelie continued down the street picking up her phone. As she called Mona she prepared herself to scream at her for her betrayal.

"I can't believe you would set me on a date with that monster of a man." Amelie said as Mona answered.

"Amelie I told you that it was a favor for Bill. He just lost his wife and needs a confidence boost." Mona asked pleading.

"Is that what I am to you? A confidence boost?" Amelie hung up violently. Anger rose from within her. A favor to Mona's husband? How unbelievable.

This date was supposed to get her back out into the dating world. Amelie's last boyfriend, Nathan had left a horrible abyss within her that no amount of shopping could fill. This date was meant to be a distraction for her, not a favor to Mona's idiot husband Bill. Amelie fumed even more thinking about Nathan and the missed opportunity of a night off. She walked the streets of New York aimlessly, stomping her pumps. The ring of Amelie's phone almost made her jump out of her porcelain skin. She was happy for the chance to tell Mona where she could shove her blind date.

"Mona I don't want to speak to you right now. I can't believe you." Amelie said as she went to shut the phone again. A man's voice surprised her as it came through.

"Is this Amelie Rose, daughter of Raquel and Samuel Rose?" The man's voice sounded apologetic.

"Yes." Amelie said with extraordinary pride for her wealthy, successful parents. It was normal for newspapers and magazines to call asking for interviews about the corporate power couple.

"Miss Rose, I'll need you to come down to your parent's home at your earliest convenience. The sooner the better." The man other end of the phone hung up.

    Amelie jogged to the side of the street and hailed down a cab. She had the driver rush to her parent's home on Park Avenue. Thoughts of what awaited her when she arrived got her excited. She hadn't seen her parents in about two months and her twenty first birthday was just around the corner. Perhaps it was a surprise party or an elegant soiree. She thought, hoping for something dazzling. When she arrived, she wasn't greeted by servers dressed tastefully, or acrobats on the lawn that were paid by her parents. There were no decorations or music either. Instead, she was greeted by grief and agony that struck her heart. There, the mansion that Amelie had grown up in was burnt down completely. Smoke hung in the still air above the house, and fire trucks were parked close, as police officers talked to neighbors. Nothing but ash and rubble remained of her childhood home. She ran up to the gate where police officers and firemen stood talking, frantically looking for her parents. A woman with hair pulled up into a tight bun and a blazer walked up to her.

"Miss Rose, I'm so sorry to inform you, but there were no survivors of the fire. Your parents were inside the house when it ignited." Amelie's knees and purse hit the hard pavement and she let out a shrill scream as her entire world crashed around her.

People walked around her as she cried and cursed god. Mona's pearlescent Cadillac pulled into the extensive drive way and she ran to her dear distraught friend. She knelt down next to Amelie and held her in her arms. Amelie cried as Mona rubbed her back and comforted her. It slowly became night and the sky turned black, stars twinkled not seeming to care about Amelie's crushed life. She still sat on the driveway in front what remained of her family's mansion and rocked herself in Mona's soft arms.

"Sweetheart, let's get you home. Here's your phone." Mona finally spoke as she helped her devastated friend up. She slipped a phone that was laying in the driveway into Amelie's handbag along with the contents that had spilt onto the driveway.

Amelie nodded as Mona helped her into her Cadillac. Bill silently drove Amelie and Mona to Amelie's apartment across town. None of them said anything, but Amelie did what she could to not look at Mona who was flashing sympathetic big brown eyes toward her. Amelie hated feeling pitied. It made her feel vulnerable and weak. She looked out the cars tinted window and did everything she could to not break down again. Her breath was hard to catch, and she squeezed her eyes tightly. The tall white building with layered balconies appeared out the window, and Amelie took a deep breath. The same place that Amelie called home for the past three years suddenly felt unfamiliar. She wanted nothing but her parents and her childhood home. She wished to go back and accept her mother's offer to live with them, but remembered how she insisted to be on her own.

"Are you going to be okay tonight dear?" Mona asked, putting a delicate hand on her back. Amelie left the car as she slammed the door and went into the apartment without responding. She didn't understand her anger toward Mona but she was glad to have somewhere to direct it. The Cadillac drove off into the night and Amelie wanted to scream at them not to leave her alone. Instead, she walked up the stoop and into the building, holding her head high.

Her luxurious apartment had never felt so empty and baron as she unlocked and opened the door. Amelie turned on the lights and took the single photo that hung off the hallway wall. She took it into her bedroom with her, holding it tightly. She passed an art easel with the same unfinished, and untouched painting that had sat there for over a year. All the walls were white and it hadn't really looked like anyone lived there. There were no decorations or photographs besides the one in her trembling hand. She unzipped her black dress and let it fall to the floor before kicking off her pumps and threw her handbag onto the side of her bed. All that remained on her toned, tanned body was her red and black lace lingerie that Nathan had given her before she found him cheating with the elementary school teacher. She wished the underwear hadn't been so appealing so she could throw it away and forget about that asshole. She shook the thought of Nathan from her mind and crawled under the feather down Duvet and on top of the silk sheets, and turned on the plain tableside lamp. She held the photo up to her chest and then looked at it. The photo was taken almost ten years ago today. It beautifully portrayed her parents and she on her eleventh birthday in front of what was now their charred tomb. Amelie let the hot tears streak through her carefully done make up as she remembered her wonderful childhood. She thought of the horseback riding her mother and her loved to do together and the golf she enjoyed with her father. Her heart was overcome by the feeling of guilt as she thought about all the time that had passed since she last saw her beloved parents. She ached inside to have that time back with them, that time to love and cherish them like they deserved. Amelie knew time was the one thing that she could never get back no matter how much money she had or how hard she worked. Pain and agony flooded her body, it was followed by the sensation that it was all a dream. The day had been so bizarre it couldn't have been real. The throbbing ache that Amelie felt was so sever, it couldn't be real. Sleep captured her to that thought, that none of it had happened.

Chapter 2: A Change of Heart

    The next day, Amelie woke up next to the photo. Bleeding mascara was dried onto her face and also her memory foam pillow. She clumsily reached for her cell phone to call her mother, she desperately wanted to hear the voicemails her mother had left her, each one saying 'I love you" at the end of it. She dug through her purse to find the silver smartphone. As she unlocked it, she didn't recognize the background as hers. The photo was of a big brown dog with curly fur and giant loving brown eyes. Amelie recognized it as a Chesapeake lab. Her dream dog. The kind of dog that would love you through heaven and hell, and always be by your side. She giggled through tears as she looked at the goofy face of the adorable dog. She wished her home had been big enough to have capacity for a companion like the one in the background of the phone, but it wasn't even big enough for a pet goldfish. Alas, she chose her current apartment because it offered a short walk to work and the amenities. When she had bought it, she thought about the inspiration for painting that the apartment offered. It was silent and her neighbors were almost never home. She regretted it as she thought about the old painting beside the balcony window that had been sitting, and the fact that she hadn't even seen the building's pool or tennis court. Amelie unlocked the phone's screen and glanced around what it had to offer. She opened the photo album and glimpsed through them, feeling a bit mischievous as she did it. The first picture was the one of the lab. He was on the end of a kayak on an open lake. The photo was beautiful and reminded Amelie of the easy going life she used to crave. A fishing pole sat off to the side of the dog and a big beautiful blue house sat in the background. Amelie opened up the file name. 'Zeus and I fishing." The photo read. The name Zeus matched the large goofy looking dog. Amelie allowed her finger to swipe left to the next photo. This photo was a breathtaking view of Watkin's Glen State Park here in New York. The photo looked like heaven. Amelie longed for the day she could visit that exact spot, and enjoy that exact view not through a screen. She had planned to take a few weeks off of work to admire the park last year but she had never gotten the chance between advertising jobs. She had been trying for years to become partner at her agency and hoped last year it would happen. It still hadn't. Amelie sighed and sat up in bed. She felt soiled from sleeping in yesterday's clothing and not bathing last night. She removed the lace lingerie and threw them on top of the designer dress that still sat on the floor and she made her way to the bathroom, taking the photo and the phone with her.

    The cold tile burned Amelie's small feet as she shuffled onto it. She looked into the medicine cabinet mirror and felt even worse about herself. A false eyelash barely hung on to her once precisely made up eye, and the other was stuck in her smeared eyebrow. She removed them and took a white remover wipe to her face and stained it. Her naked face still

felt grimy and oily from the entire night of letting it seep into her skin. Amelie walked over to her Jacuzzi bathtub and allowed the water to warm up and steam the entire room. The warm steam opened up her face and calmed her nerves as she closed her eyes tightly, warding off the tears and the thoughts. She held a bottle of lavender oil above the bath and watched as a few drops to fell in. She added bubbles and let them foam to the top before she looked around for her regular book that she read when she bathed when the stranger's phone caught her eye. Amelie unlocked it again and went back to the photo album as she sank into the warm bath water, careful not to submerge it. The third picture in the phone was of Amelie's favorite bookstore. She noticed that in the window was a flyer for a book signing by her favorite Author. Amelie felt a sudden and deep attraction to the owner of the phone. They we're living the life that Amelie had first set out to live, the life that work got in the way of. Amelie closed out of the photo album and looked around, hoping to find traces of regret in their life like she had in hers. She opened and App named "Journal" and felt sure that she would find what she was looking for there. Damning evidence that they didn't lead a perfect life. The first was from two days ago and it read;
"July 19th
I'm spending another long night in the fire station. Tonight we ate spaghetti and it painfully reminded me of Joliette. Nights like tonight are almost unbearably lonely. I sleep in a bunk

with ten other men that I consider friends, and still I'm lonely. Lately, I've been questioning if becoming a firefighter after the accident was really the best choice. That fire had taken so much away from me, including Joliette. All I wanted was to feel some sort of control over the flames. Now I regret it. Every fire I see reminds me of that night that we laid in bed for the last time. She was in my arms when I smelled the smoke. I do everything that I can to shake what happened next from my memory. I tried to save her. God knows I did."

    Tears fell from Amelie's face and into the bath. The pain from the entry matched her agony of her own heart. She felt every emotion that had been so toxic and defeating. She began to drown in the pain and grief that her parents left behind when they died. She put the phone by the bath and submerged herself into the now cold water. She began to plead with god to help it go away, but nothing helped. The sore open wound in her heart still gushed from the absence. She pushed the drain down with her foot and allowed all of the water to wash down it. She laid naked and wet in the empty tub and cradled herself. Enough time passed to dry all the water from her skin when she got up the strength to stand and dry herself off with the white plush towel. She returned to the bed and removed the towel. Her long wet blonde hair drenched and cooled the pillow behind her head as she laid herself down. She again, picked up the phone. She went to music library app in the phone, and again felt the connection again. Bands such as 'The

Beatles' littered the list of music that Amelie and the stranger had both loved. Amelie felt strange as she immersed herself in the emotion. She felt something for the phone's owner and she still had yet to see him, speak to him or touch him. She wished the man had photos of himself on the phone so she could know his face, and look into his eyes. When she pictured him, she saw a tall, muscular man in a firefighter's suit. He had a handsome face and dark perfect hair. His eyes were blue and loving. Eventually, Amelie slipped into a dream. She dreamt of the man and his heroic life. In her sleep, she dreamt that he saved her from her parents from the fire that took them from her. He then kissed her passionately on the lips and embraced her against his strong body. He played with her hair and he smelled of rosemary and eucalyptuses. Her mother spoke in the dream and Amelie woke up eager to see her when her eyes shot open. She woke up only to the empty apartment, the strange phone buzzing. She opened it hoping for it to be the owner.
"Hello?" She asked, a bit groggy.
"I believe you have my phone." The voice said laughing. Amelie sat up in bed, excited to be speaking to the man that invaded her dreams, that was slowly patching her heart.
"I do. I'm sorry I picked it up by accident." Amelie said as her heart raced.
"Well, that's okay. I'm always misplacing it." He laughed again. A voice in the background egged him on for something.

"Would you be willing to bring it to a steakhouse? Tomorrow at eight? Maybe, we can even grab a bite to eat." The voice sounded nervous but hopeful. The second voice said something in auditable in an excited tone. "Excuse my friend." The man said, embarrassed.

"That sounds great. Just tell me where." The man proceeded to give Amelie the directions.

Amelie sat up and felt something besides grief for once since her loss. She was washed over with giddiness and excitement by the man's words. She ran the conversation through her head repeatedly, getting more and more enthusiastic about the date. She went to her closet and dug through the massive amounts of designer clothes, and suddenly knew where all of her travel money went. She sat on the bed again and cried. She realized that it wasn't for her parents this time, but for the time and money she had wasted on such trivial things. The life the man on the phone had was the one she wanted to live. He didn't let loss or anything for that matter stand in the way of his happiness or his dreams. He enjoyed the real things in life, while she wasted them on superficial things like clothes. Regret washed over her now for how she treated the man in the coffee house. He was polite and looked like he needed to catch a break, she of course threw that out the window. If he were anything like the firefighter that was the phone owner, he was a brave, honorable man whom deserved more. Her regret got the best of her and

Amelie decided to call Mona, after realizing how she had treated her also.

"Hello?" Mona asked as she answered the phone, obviously concerned and cautious.

"Mona, I just wanted to apologize for the way I acted. I had no right to feel like I was worth more than that man, and I had no right to treat you like that either. Amelie felt guilty for the surprise in her friend's voice.

"Um, wow Amelie, that's okay. I would have you call Parker so you could apologize to him but I don't have his number." Amelie sighed, she did want to apologize to Parker.

Amelie hung up the phone after saying her goodbyes, feeling like she had re-patched the friendship to some degree. The hurt of rejection was evident on the man's disfigured face, and it was not eating at her for putting it there. Sleep once again consumed Amelie, this time there was no one to rescue her or her parents. Instead, she found herself in the flames again. The hot flames of eternal hell fire completely surrounded her. She sat in a glass cage as everyone whom she had ever wronged walked by her pointing and laughing at her burns. At the end of the line, her parents walked by. Her mother stood, stunning as always, her father looked dignified. They stood there, shaking their heads at their daughter. The hell fire stopped, but a new pain of knowing she disappointed them consumed her. Her mother Raquel spoke.

"This isn't the way we raised you Amelie." Her mother said, displeasure in her eyes.

"Where did we go wrong?" Her father asked as he shrugged.

The two of them disappeared as Amelie woke up from the nightmare in a hot sweat. She screamed and kicked her blanket. She screamed louder as her parent's disappointed faces burned in her mind.

"I'm sorry!" She screamed to the heavens, burring her face into her hands.

Amelie's raw eyes didn't allow for her to cry anymore. She laid on her side as the phone caught her vision. Curiosity and a desperate need for a distraction took over as Amelie flipped through the phone. She looked through the photos again. This time, she made it to the photos of his home. It was the same beautiful blue three story home with white plantation shutters that was in the back ground of the boat picture. The lawn was huge and a swing hung from the huge tree out front. 'No wonder he sleeps in the fire house, there's no way this is anywhere near the city.' Amelie thought to herself as she was admiring the home. A wrap around porch caught Amelie's eye. She envied how it would make a beautiful place to paint. Amelie looked at the time on the phone and her heart stopped.

"Noon!" She cursed at herself for losing track of time.

She began to look for the perfect dress and shoes for the date, this time not letting her regret the money she spent on her wardrobe. When she was satisfied and dressed, she went to the hairdresser that her mother used to take her to. She stepped out into the daylight for the first time in a week and the sun burned her sensitive deprived eyes as it greeted her. She walked to the nearest hairdresser, attempting to fake pride as she did. The woman inside the small shop all gave her a sympathetic look as she walked in the door. Ammonia hung in the air, and Amelie tried to focus on that so the tears didn't invade her once again.

"So sorry to hear about your parent's Hun. Your mama was really a great lady." The owner said sitting her down in a black swivel chair and pulling a cape over her. All Amelie could return was a weak smile. "Let us do your makeup too. On the house." The woman said as she began to play with Amelie's long blonde hair that hadn't been washed in days.

 Amelie looked at herself as the woman worked. She saw that dark bags under her eyes, and the acne that began to break out on her ivory complexion from days of not maintaining herself. Amelie sighed, disappointed in herself for letting her appearance fall to the wayside. She felt even worse remembering that she had let her character dissolve into a self-centered, stuck up narcissist. As the woman finished, Amelie's hair hung in beautiful curls and a flawless face of makeup help her recognize herself again. Amelie didn't feel as great as she normally did after dolling herself up, she hoped it was a positive thing noting change. She looked back down at the phone just to see Zeus. The time blazed at her. It was already seven o' clock by the time they finished. Amelie stood and paid before hailing a taxi. Excitement welled within her as she did. She showed the address to the cab driver that the phone owner had given her and they were off. She pulled up to a beautiful steak house that was lit stunningly by what looked like candles. She walked in and took a booth from the hostess. Time past and eight came and went. Amelie thought about how the man's time wasn't more important than hers, and he being a few minutes late wasn't the end of the world. She had decided what she wanted and had drank two glasses of red wine by the time her date walked in. She thought back to how many hobbies and interests they shared. The man turned and Amelie was shocked to see that it was Parker. He walked over to Amelie smiling wide.

"It's so great to see you! I wanted to apologize to you Amelie." Amelie couldn't find her voice as it squeezed her throat shut.

"No, Parker, I need to apologize to you." She managed to choke out.

"Please let me. Amelie, I had no idea that was your parent's fire. I'm so sorry for your loss and if I had known, I wouldn't have asked you to stay at the coffee house." Parker said sitting across from her.

"That's actually why I wanted to apologize." Amelie choked out.

"Oh please Amelie. Please, don't apologize." He said, not understanding what she was trying to say. "What brings you here tonight?" He asked before she could say more.

"Actually, I'm returning a phone I found." Parker let out an amazing chuckle as she said it and held up the phone.

"No kidding? Well, I believe you have my cell phone. Did I leave it at the coffee house?" Amelie was awe struck.

"Um, no. I found it at my parent's house. In the yard." She said, thinking about what that meant. "So you were one of the firemen? That put it out?"

"I'm sorry I thought Bill or Mona told you." He said as he sat across from her.

"They didn't. We're my parents? Never mind." She trailed off as she sipped her wine and looked out the window. Not wanting to let him see the pain in her eyes.

"No, they weren't awake." He answered, putting his hand on hers. "You owe me a date." He said changing the subject and smiling, not wanting her to cry. Amelie smiled at Parker and pushed the menu toward him.

"So, did you go through my phone?" He asked, looking at the menu.

"Zeus is cute." It was all she said before she smiled and winked at him.

The evening continued as the two talked about everywhere Parker had traveled. Amelie was thoroughly enjoying herself with another man for the first time since

Nathan had left. She didn't think about her parents or her regrets while she was with Parker. She only enjoyed herself. The burns on his face no longer made her cringe. She saw them for what they were. A badge of honor and a reminder of loss.

"I would love to see your home in person." Amelie confessed after Parker mentioned it with pride.

"Are you sure? It's quite a drive." Parker asked while Amelie nodded.

"I'm sure. Could I stay the night if we go? It's so late." The two left the steakhouse and drove the long drive to the beautiful home after Parker agreed to let her stay.

"After my home burnt down, I lost myself in building this. It's my dream home."

"Mine too." Amelie accidently let out.

"Can I show you around?" He asked pulling up to the massive home. Amelie nodded, tickled by the offer.

He took her through the giant white French doors, and Zeus immediately greeted them, tail wagging. Parker introduced them and he warmed up to Amelie immediately as she rubbed his tummy. The first room they came to was the massive foyer. Freshly cut sweet peas danced in a vase under a huge mirror. Amelie looked to the side to see a huge living room with Victorian couches and a massive fire place. Parker led her to the kitchen that was rustically decorated and smelled like chocolate chip cookies. The only thing left was his bedroom Amelie realized, feeling nervous. Parker instead took her by the hand and led her up to the art room. It was amazing and took Amelie's breath away. Huge canvases hung on the teal walls. Sculptures sat on desks and art supplies were organized everywhere. It inspired Amelie to her very core as she saw all it had to offer.

"Do you want to watch a movie maybe?" Parker said seeing the emotion in her eyes.

"I would love too." She said holding his burned hand.

Parker led her down the stairs and into the foyer. Amelie watched as he grabbed a blanket from the living room and rejoined her, grabbing her hand again. He led her outside and she admired the moonlight that was bouncing off the lake. Parker laid the blanket down underneath the large tree that Amelie had spent so long admiring. He motioned Amelie to sit on the blanket and he pulled a large screen from off the house. He went into a small shed and pulled out an old projector and a laptop. He set up the movie 'The Notebook' with his laptop and used the projector to make it the size of a theater screen on the hose. He rejoined her on the blanket as the movie started. Amelie laid next to Parker looking at him. She knew so much about the man. She was overcome with an emotion so strong, she grabbed his shoulders and kissed him deeply. He didn't pull away, or flinch, he only kissed her back. He tasted so sweet and creamy. He held her head with his arm, cradling her delicately. She felt so safe and secure in his shaped arms.

So many emotions hit her at once, and Amelie, besides her best efforts, began to cry.

"I know. I know it's hard." Parker said holding her in his arms. "It will be okay." For the first time in her life, Amelie felt safe. She felt like it was going to be okay just because he said it would be. She hugged Parker back and he held her tight and rolled over, pointing at the sky. "Your parents aren't gone Amelie. They're always watching after you and keeping you safe."

"Do you want to know how I know that's true?" Parker looked at her and smiled, nodding his head. "Because, they lead me to you." Parker smiled and grabbed Amelie into his arms.

He carried her up into the bedroom and laid her down. He laid her onto the hand quilted comforter, and laid beside her. They looked into each other's eyes, smiling at each other, feeling the butterflies inside them flutter simultaneously. The both drifted to sleep with each other's face in their minds. Amelie woke up to the smell of bacon and Zeus lightly sniffing her toes. There was a moment of disorientation as she looked to the pewter walls and unfamiliar room. Parker showed up in the doorway with a breakfast tray, he smiled and brought it to her. On the tray was a glass of orange juice, a bowl of fruits, bacon and eggs. Beside those was a brochure for Venice, Italy.

"Every year I take a trip. I normally stay in the states, but tomorrow I'm going to Italy." Parker said, sitting next to Amelie in bed.

"Wow! Venice? I've always wanted to go." Amelie said excitedly eating a piece of fruit.

"So, you'll go with me?" Parker said smiling, excited.

"Well, I do have my bereavement leave, but I mean we just met." Amelie saw Parker's heartbreak as she denied him.

"I know Amelie. I also know that you feel this too. This physical need to be together. This connection." Parker held Amelie's trembling hand.

"Parker, you're right I do feel it." Parker perked up as she looked at him.

"You'll go with me? Please say you'll go with me. This is a trip of a life time, I don't want you to regret missing the opportunity." The pleading in Parker's eyes was impossible to say no to.

"Okay, Parker. I'd love to go with you to Italy." Parker kissed Amelie deeply and let her eat her breakfast as they talked about how exciting the trip was sure to be.

Chapter 3: The Perfect Ending

Amelie rumbled through her closet looking for what to wear to Italy. She went through sun dresses, tank tops and shorts. Excitement and delight pulsed through her veins. As she grabbed her camera, she saw the picture of her parents laying on the bed. As she picked it up and held it close to her body, she didn't cry. She only wanted to make them happy and live her life without any regrets the words Parker had said hanging in her ears. She put the photo with the rest of her belongings she was planning to take to Italy, and zipped up the bag. Parker came in from the living room and stood in the threshold of the bedroom.

"Are you ready beautiful?" He asked, placing his hand on her hip.

"I'm ready." She said as she kissed his lips.

The flight to Italy was utterly breathtaking as they flew over Venice. Beautiful buildings stood tall as people hurried between them, enjoying their days. Parker complimented Amelie on her beautiful appearance for the hundredth time as they landed in the serene village.

"So beautiful." Amelie said looking around at the Tuscany Village.

"I couldn't agree more." Parker said, only looking at her.

The two ventured the streets of Italy for almost two hours before deciding on having lunch at a tiny café. Parker ordered them both lobster Linguini in Italian before he got down on one knee. He pulled out a small velvet box and held it up to Amelie.

"Amelie, I have no interest on wasting my life. I think that me spending any longer without you as my wife would be a waste of my breath. Please, make me the happiest man in Italy, and say yes." The bright diamond shone in the sun. Amelie gasped and stood up utterly shocked and surprised. She wanted to be his wife also, so desperately.

"Yes Parker, yes!" She screamed as bystanders looked on laughing at her loveable reaction.

Parker stood, and slid the ring on to her finger before kissing her hard and spinning her around. Her yellow sundress spun around her and people clapped and Amelie kissed Parker feeling alive for the very first time.

"I love you Amelie."

"I love you too Parker."

THE END

Large And In Charge
Kathleen Hope

Table of Contents

Chapter 1: Traumatic Beginnings

Chapter 2: The Funeral

Chapter 3: Five Years Later

Chapter 4: A Wedding

Chapter 5: A Recycled Past

Chapter 6: Trial and Error

Chapter 1: Traumatic Beginnings

Luna Archer's entire world was about to crash and burn around her, but she sat unknowingly enjoying a freshly brewed cup of coffee and a chocolate biscotti. She placed a hand delicately on her pregnant belly with a smile. In this moment, her world was the best that it had ever been. She was going to have Damian Archer's child. The man that she met at the tender age of fourteen and had loved every day since then. Her husband was due back soon from Japan where he was working as an Army Medic. Luna knew that what Damian was doing in Japan had been exceptionally draining, but it was even more rewarding, he had reassured her countless times that what he was doing was safe, that there was no reason for her to worry. Luna played with her short caramel hair as she looked for baby names. She flipped through the book with a smile. She had insisted to keep the gender of the baby unknown, wanting it to be a surprise. The excitement mounted more and more every day, and at forty weeks of pregnancy, Luna was ready to meet her new baby.

A hearty knock came at Luna's front door. It hadn't been a long walk from the small kitchen to the front door, but still her heart raced as she anticipated her husband's presence. She opened the door and broke her own heart in one swift move. Standing at the door hadn't been her husband ready to take her up in his muscular arms, but it was two men dressed in decorated Navy uniforms. They held an American flag that had been folded in a triangle and placed in a shadow box. Luna's welcoming smile fell into a heartbroken look of agony. The first and taller man spoke with a soft and delicate voice. The looks on their faces had also been contorted into a sorrowful and regretful frown.

"Miss Luna Archer, we regretfully inform you that the honorable Damian Archer has been found, deceased." The man looked like the words were acid in his mouth, and just letting them pass his lips was monumentally painful.

Luna fell to her knees as the pain of losing the man that she loved more than the air that she breathed settled in. Her heart shattered and her world burned as she was handed the flag. The men stood there without a word as the woman before them became broken. They looked at each other and left Luna there to struggle for air through the insufferable pain that she felt. The pain that she felt was not only heartbreak, but also labor. She screamed for the men to come back to her as her water broke. The two Navy officers to her ran back and helped her to her feet. They hurriedly helped the agonized Luna into their vehicle and drove her to the hospital to give birth to her now fatherless child. Her world was like a nightmare. She couldn't allow herself to let the fact that her husband was now dead sink in. It was too unbearable. When they reached the Cedar City hospital, a nurse came running out, wheelchair in hand, ready to admit Luna. An hour later, she was in the delivery room, giving birth to her child. The two men who had delivered the news of her husband's death stood in the room. The first one had been exceptionally handsome. His skin was darker, like he had been of Hispanic descent. He had short black hair and a warm smile. His face was a mixture of young but distinguished, he was all around nice to look at. The second was a shorter man with acne scars that had pitted his skin. He looked around like he was out of his element in the birthing room. His hair was also dark, but was shaved so that it was barely visible. Luna let out a scream as another contraction hit her. She was rethinking her decision to pass up on the epidural as the pain made her want to pass out. A young and beautiful nurse came into the room and checked her dilation.

"I hope you're ready to push." She said with a smile before going and grabbing Luna's doctor. The shorter man watched the nurse as she left but the taller one kept an eye on Luna. The look in his eyes was hard to explain. He looked like he was keeping some sort of deep secret.

Luna's doctor walked into the room and began Luna's voyage to motherhood. The pain was ungodly as she let out another scream. The taller man walked over to her and held her hand. The nametag on his uniform said Abraham. Luna took his hand and squeezed it while she pushed and looked into his mysterious blue eyes. She let out another loud scream as her baby girl was born. The doctor handed Luna her child and

Luna was washed over with the strongest love that she had ever felt. The baby opened her eyes to revel a face that duplicated her father's. Luna wanted to cry at the resemblance. A nurse took her and began to clean the new baby off while Luna took a breath. She looked at Abraham.

"What's your name?" Luna asked, wanting to know if the man had known her husband.

"Jonathan. Jonathan Abraham." Luna recognized the name immediately. Jonathan had been a dear friend to Damion while he wasn't at home.

"Jonathan, what happened to my husband?" Luna was covered in sweat and her body was exhausted, but she hadn't forgotten about Damion. Jonathan looked at the shorter man as he shook his head.

"Suicide." Luna couldn't believe what she had heard. Damion was not the kind of man to take his life. He wasn't the kind to leave his wife and new baby behind in a selfish and permanent act. The look on Luna's face betrayed what she was thinking before the nurse brought her new baby in to the room and laid her on her chest.

"Do you have a name for the little angel?" The nurse asked sweetly.

"Oh, that's right." Luna had to think. She thought about Damion's mother who had dies five years ago from cancer. The name fit the beautiful little girl. Damion had looked just like his mother and his daughter had looked just like him.

"Meadow Anne Archer."

Chapter 2: The Funeral

Luna watched as Meadow played with her hair. She smiled at her mother with love as the tears fell down her mother's beautiful face. Luna wore a long black dress that was meant for the funeral. She topped it off with a large black brimmed hat and a birdcage veil to hide her face. Meadow wore a black onesie, seeing as there wasn't much else that a one week old child could have worn to her father's funeral. Jonathan sat next to the pair as he prepared everything that he could for the funeral. Luna had been exceptionally thankful for his help. The shorter man whose name was Andy Ancon had left the day after he delivered the news, but Jonathan couldn't just leave the newly widowed, new mother that was his dearest friend's wife.

"We had better get going." Jonathan said as he put a soft hand on Luna's back. She smiled at him and he helped her up and out to the limo that he had set up for her.

That Catholic Church that they had planned for the funeral was enormous, and it needed to be. Over 500 people came to grieve the loss of the amazing and honorable man. The Navy had been nice enough to pay for the costs of the funeral, something else that Luna had been thankful for. Large stained glass windows lined the walls of the old building and pictured images of Mary the patron saint. A closed casket sat at the front of the room, almost buried in bundles of flowers and letters, all belonging to Damion. The sight of her husband's casket was almost too much for Luna to handle. Candles lit the old church and a sorrow hung in the air as a priest walked to the front and began to honor Damion's life with prayers.

Jonathan walked up next in his decorated uniform. He bowed his head and took in a deep breath.

"Damion Archer was an amazing man. A man with heart and soul. He was the kind of man to do anything and everything for everyone else, letting himself fall behind. He leaves behind an amazing woman and a beautiful baby girl. Damion and I spent a lot of time together, and let me tell you that he loved his wife. She was the beat to his heart and the light to his soul. Today, the world becomes a less fortunate place as we lay this wonderful man to rest." Jonathan saluted the casket and returned to his seat next to Luna. Luna stood and held her eulogy in her shaking hands with tears in her eyes.

"I met Damion when I was fourteen. We met at the public library, here in town. I was checking out a book that he was reading. I had reserved it." Luna couldn't help herself as sobs came from her chest. "He was nice enough to let me read it with him." Luna pulled the old book from her purse and kissed it before putting it onto her husband's casket. She cleared her throat and began again. "Meadow is facing a horrible loss by not being able to have her father in her life, but I hope she grows up with his spirit and his love near her." Luna couldn't speak any longer and gave into her pain. She screamed and hit her knees in heartbreak. People looked to each other and whispered as they let her sit there in agony. Jonathan was the only one to come to her rescue. He grabbed her arm, but before she left, she said just a bit more. "I love you Damion."

The rest of the funeral floated on without much notice from Luna. She did what she could to speak to people and be social. The pity in their eyes was next to unbearable. She wanted to run to the casket and to join her beloved to spend all of eternity with him, but she resisted for the sake of Meadow. As people filed out of the church, Luna sat at a pew in the very last row. Meadow sat near her in a car seat, smiling at her mother. Luna rested her head into her arm and began to cry. She felt a soft but heavy hand on her shoulder and she looked up. Jonathan sat there with a kind look on his face. An older man walked past them, a man that Luna hadn't recognized. He tipped his hat to Jonathan and continued to the casket, placing a note and a medal onto it. The man disappeared as quickly as he had come.

"That was a beautiful eulogy." Luna said as she wiped her eyes. "Thank you for it."

Jonathan said nothing but he comforted her with his eyes before helping her up and holding meadow. The three of them walked out of the church together.

That night, Luna sat up in her bed. Meadow was in the crib next to her and Jonathan had been staying in the guest bedroom. She thought about all of the food that covered her kitchen, and couldn't help but feel hungry. She made her way to the kitchen in nothing but one of Damion's shirts and a pair of cotton panties. She screamed when she saw Jonathan sitting at her kitchen table. He covered his eyes and went to walk back to his room.

"Wait, Jonathan." Luna begged.

"Yes ma'am?" Jonathan said, still covering his eyes.

"How did he die?" She had needed to know.

"He cut his wrists ma'am." Jonathan said with sorrow.

That was impossible. Her husband had been a man that became very sick when he saw his own blood. He would have passed out long before the possibility of killing himself became possible.

"Stay here." Luna demanded.

Luna returned to her room to put on pajama pants before she came running back, the thoughts that were running through her head demanded to be answered. She came back out of the room, careful not to wake Meadow. She sat down at the table with Jonathan, his eyes looked bewildered.

"Look, this is the last letter that he sent me." Luna said as she gave the letter to Jonathan. He read it over. The letter talked about how excited he was to meet his new baby and how home was the only thing on his mind. "Does this look like something that a suicidal man would write?" Luna said as she bit at her nails.

"Luna, Damion didn't commit suicide." Jonathan admitted shaking his head.

The words stunned Luna and forced her to stay silent even though questions pounded in her head and in her heart. She had known that Damion wouldn't have done something like that, he wouldn't have just abandoned her like that. He had been so excited to be a father. He beamed with it whenever he looked at Luna's belly. He would put his hand on her stomach and speak softly to his unborn child. Jonathan spoke after too long of a silence.
"He knew too much Luna. They murdered him." Jonathan said looking around.
"Who?" Luna begged.
"The Navy, well scientists that were with the Navy. They had been practicing unethical experiments on Japanese civilians. They made it look like a suicide, but Luna, you can't say anything. They're watching you." The thought sent Luna back into her seat. It had been inconceivable. Luna, without anything else to do, vomited into the kitchen rubbish bin. She held her head and began to cry. Jonathan stood and held her. "We'll figure this out." Luna had no other option but to believe him. Doing otherwise, meant drowning in grief or regret.
"I need to know everything." Luna said wiping her mouth.
"Damion was working closely with some really awful people Luna. They did things like deprive innocent people of all human contact, for years. Damion was chosen to be the medic

who evaluated them. You have to know, that there was no way that he could have gotten out of it. It was either do what they said, or they were going to kill you, and Meadow."

"They killed him. Why did they kill him?" Luna asked.

"He knew too much. He was a liability. What they're doing is against every law and code." Jonathan answered.

"What can I do?" Luna asked helplessly.

"We are going to catch them. With the evidence that we gather, there's no way that they can walk innocently. Are you willing to do this?" Jonathan asked.

"Anything for Damion." Luna said, her heart pounding.

"Luna, one more thing. Andy is working for them. Don't let him know that anything's up okay?"

"Okay." Luna walked back to her room in shock.

Chapter 3: Five Years Later

Luna anxiously awaited Jonathan. She had baked him his favorite, apple pie with vanilla bean ice cream and chocolate pudding. She had spent hours getting ready that morning and had spent so much time on perfecting her hair and her dress. For the first time in a long time, she felt beautiful and in love. Jonathan had been working with her for five years to find justice for her late husband Damion's murder. In that time together, they had begun to fall in love. Since he had no family, when Jonathan came home, he came home to Luna and Meadow. Meadow loved Jonathan so much that he was the love of her life. She asked countless times if Jonathan was her father, even though Luna always told her no, she called him daddy anyway. Secretly, both Luna and Jonathan had loved when the little five year old would run up to him with her arms open and her eyes wide, calling for her daddy. Luna watched as his red car came pulling into the driveway. She smiled as she called Meadow. Her beautiful five year old came running into the Kitchen and into her mother's arms. Jonathan opened the front door with a huge smile and a hug for Meadow. He hugged Luna with one arm and kissed her on the cheek.
"Hello, you two." Jonathan said as he put his things away.
"Go look in the kitchen." Luna said with a smile.
Jonathan turned the corner and let out a gasp of excitement. The Navy didn't feed well, he would always say. Luna and

Meadow joined him at the breakfast table and enjoyed the dessert for lunch. They talked about the ongoing things of their lives, and how Meadow was going to join kindergarten next year. The thought upset Luna deeply. Meadow had been with Luna every day since her birth, and being away for even a day seemed dreadful.

That night after they put Meadow to bed, Luna and Jonathan met at their usual place at the kitchen table. They gathered more evidence against the Navy. They had a pretty tight case and any judge with a brain would rule in their favor. The only thing they had to be sure of was that they didn't let anyone in to what they were doing. That kind of information in the wrong hands would have been disastrous. After five years, they had finally completed their case.

"Want to celebrate?" Jonathan asked as he grabbed a bottle of champagne.

"Are you kidding? Of course I do." Luna grabbed two glasses and filled them up.

Jonathan poured two large glasses of the champagne while Luna watched him. He wasn't obligated to be helping her. Helping her meant risking his life, he was doing it out of the goodness of his heart. She could no longer resist or suppress the urge to kiss him. She stood as he put his glass down and welcomed her into his arms. He breathed her in as he did. She smelled of sweet honeysuckles in summer. She looked at him with her big wide beautiful eyes. Jonathan reached down and gave her a long and lingering kiss on her thick lips. The feeling of being kissed had abandoned Luna for so long. She hadn't realized until now just how much that she had really missed it. Jonathan held her in his arms and felt his heart skip a beat as he looked at her face. Beauty radiated off of every inch of her. Jonathan kissed her again and then led her to the bedroom, carefully passing Meadow's room. He opened the door and followed her in kissing her neck as he laid her on the bed. She gave him eyes that asked him to stop. She had a pain in her stomach that told her that she was deceiving Damien. Jonathan understood without her having to say anything.

"He would have wanted you to be happy. Are you happy?" He asked.

"You know that I am Jon." Luna said.

"Then what's the problem?" He asked confused.

When she didn't answer him, Jonathan opted just to hold her, like he had done so many times before. He rested his head on hers and gently tickled her arm.

"I love you Jonathan." It had been the first time that she had ever said it.

"I love you too Luna." his hand rolled through her long hair, and he meant it.

Luna looked at Jonathan with a love that was stronger than light. He was a noble man with a big heart. His handsome face showed so much love and compassion for Luna. She put her hand delicately on his face and leaned in to kiss him deeply. His scent invaded her nose and intoxicated her all at once. A tingling overcame her and she knew that she had to be with him and that she had to be one with him. She sat up on her knees and pulled at his shirt. He helped her pull it off of his muscular body as he took off hers and kissed her from her neck down to her navel. The sensation was amazing and covered her tanned and toned body with goosebumps. He pulled off his pants and began to help her with her own as he lavished her glorious body with sweet and delicate kisses. He went lower as she let out playful moans and he teased her until she couldn't take it anymore. She begged him to complete her and stop mercilessly teasing her. He gave into her demands and positioned himself over her and entered her with a hearty thrust. Her eyes rolled back and a smile came to her face. She hadn't realized just how desperately she had been craving a man until he had overwhelmed her with his masculinity. His handsome face contorted into the look of a man pleasing a woman and then into orgasmic bliss as they both climaxed together. Jonathan pulled out of her and laid next to her satisfied body as he began to kiss her again. He held her close and she could hear his pounding heart that beat for her.

Luna woke up the next morning with the smell of bacon wafting into her nostrils. For a moment she had forgotten about the night before but all at once it came flooding back to her and she was overcome with love. She looked around for something to wear and opted for Jonathan's army jacket and a pair of panties. She made her way out to the kitchen to be greeted by a big breakfast. Jonathan kissed her and smiled at her reaction. She sat down to enjoy the divine looking meal, only to see that Jonathan had placed a diamond ring on top of a dollop of whip cream. It took her a moment to understand until Jonathan got down on one knee and kissed her hand. Without letting him say the speech he had prepared, Luna screamed yes.

    Just the thought of being Jonathan's wife was so comforting and beautiful. She thought about growing old with him and spending the rest of her life in the arms of his love and protection. She stood there in her kitchen hugging the man that she loved. It had been so long. Meadow came running across the tile and into Jonathan's arms. Luna looked at her little family and smiled.

Chapter 4: A Wedding

Luna sat getting the back of her wedding dressed laced when her wedding planner walked in. She looked her over and told her that in five minutes she would be married to Jonathan Abraham. Luna stood with a smile and checked to make sure that her pregnant belly was hidden before leaving the room and walking down the aisle to meet her new husband. Excitement filled her from within and she was ready to burst with love. He stood there gazing at her with love in his eyes and his heart.

The air was filled with excitement and joy as Luna pledged her love and her life to the man that rescued her from grief and pain. A whole new world was introduced to her. It was one that wasn't so dark, in fact it was filled with joy and light. A world where pain was numbed and she felt like herself again. People cheered as Luna kissed the man that was now her husband, and the father to her next child. The feeling was amazing. Their love together was undeniable and eternal.

A chariot that was decorated in roses and that was driven by horses pulled in front of the Church and Luna and Jonathan got in and waved goodbye to their families and Meadow who was to stay with her grandmother. They were chauffeured to the airport so they could begin their honeymoon in Bora Bora. Jonathan held his wife's hand as the plane took off and gained altitude and Luna laid her head on his shoulder, her long caramel hair cascading over his shoulder. He kissed her head and watched as the Earth got further and further away.

The island finally came into view and Jonathan woke Luna from her deep sleep and watched her smile as she saw the island getaway come into view. The smile that lit up her face and Jonathan's life was beautiful and amazing. The water below was crystal blue and the sun shone on it and lit it up to a beautiful color. The plane landed and Luna looked around. It was like problems didn't exist in this part of the world. Luna kissed Jonathan and they went to their room.

"Are you going to quit the Navy after this year?" Luna had been dying to ask, but she had tried to keep it to herself till after the wedding, not knowing how he would react.

"No? Why would I?" Jonathan asked as he put away their clothes. It had been apparent that he hadn't even thought about it.

"You know what they did to Damion." Luna said wanting to cry.

"Lunessa, that wasn't the Navy it was a group of scientists that belonged to it, I'm safe." Jonathan held her in his arms, and she wanted desperately to believe him.

Chapter 5: A Recycled Past

It had been a week since Luna and Jonathan returned from their honeymoon. Luna had missed Meadow almost too much to handle. She was more visibly pregnant than when she had left and Meadow took notice. It was time for Jonathan to go back to Japan and continue his job. Meadow and Luna kissed their new man goodbye and Luna took the time to love on her dearly missed daughter before kissing her goodnight. She laid herself in bed and shut her eyes only for them to shoot open only minutes later. She heard a man yell. In that same moment she got out of bed and dressed herself to run out her door, only to find Jonathan gripping his chest where the knife still stuck out. A white truck sped off from the scene and Luna remembered it from a distant past. He looked at his wife and held her crying face in his hand and kissed her for the last time. The light in his blue eyes slowly faded as they shut. Luna pulled the knife from his chest and held him. Her screams forced the neighbors to call the police and they came immediately. Jonathan's lifeless body was taken by EMT's and Luna was put under arrest, while her mother came and picked up Meadow. The entire thing went by so fast and Luna was confused as the officer read her rights. She did what she could just to not lose it in front of Meadow who was also screaming.
It was a long ride to the police station as she was welcomed again by the familiar feeling of losing the one that she loved.

She was smothered in Jonathan's blood and she felt in ruin. The officer pulled her out of the car and shoved her down into the chair as she screamed and demanded to know what happened, but Luna wasn't even sure herself.

Chapter 6: Trial and Error

The public defender had insisted on the raggedy old dress that made Luna look frumpy and poor. It was a tactic to make the jury see her loss. The prosecutor called Luna to the stand and it took everything for her to stand and walk the five feet. The life from her had been drained. She hadn't seen Meadow in almost a year, her son who she named after his father was taken from her after he was born in prison and both her husband's laid dead in early graves.

"So, Mrs. Archer. The forensic team have come to a conclusion. That conclusion is that after your husband, Damion Archer killed himself, you went insane. This caused you to tempt Jonathan Abraham to have sex with you, impregnate you and then stab him. Is this correct?" He was a tall man with a dark head of hair and an evil smile. She knew that the Navy had been paying him off.

"No. Jonathan and I were legally married. We have a wedding certificate and witnesses. We were working to prove that The Navy was responsible for Damion's death." She knew that she had sounded crazy.

"Your kitchen knife was found buried in Jonathan's chest, with your prints all over it. Oh, and there's no documented license of your supposed marriage, and we couldn't find anyone to agree that you got married." The prosecutor said with his smile.

"That's because the Navy threatened them, and I pulled the knife from his chest." Luna said putting her head into her hands.

"As you can see your honor, this woman is devastated and had lost touch with reality. She belongs in an asylum. She's been through so much." The judge and the jury agreed. When the doors of the court room flew open, the entire court room gasped. Everyone but Luna looked up to see the intruder.

"Your honor, I'm sorry for the intrusion, but as you can see, Luna didn't kill me. I'm alive and well." Jonathan's voice had lit up Luna's life. He had been another year older and was being followed by FBI agents. "I agree, she is devastated. Thanks to Andy Ancon." An FBI agent pulled him from the spectators and put handcuffs on him along with ten other men, who had to of been the other scientists. Jonathan tossed a folder on the judge's desk. Luna ran to her husband and embraced him. "You see sir, I had to fake my death. Andy did really stab me, but he missed my heart big time, great job Andy." Cameras were pointed at Jonathan and the hysterical Luna. "Take them to prison men, and Luna, let's get you home to our kids." Jonathan held Luna and kissed her deeply. "I'm so sorry my love, but I couldn't risk your life anymore." Luna forgave him, just happy to have him in her arms.

"Case dismissed." The judge said as the officers took the men responsible for Damion's death away.

THE END

Touched In All The Right Places

Kathleen Hope

Table of Contents

Prologue: The Beginning of a Lifetime

Chapter 1: A Far Throw

Chapter 2: Striking Out

Chapter 3: Finally a Hit

Epilogue: The Perfect Game

Prologue: The Beginning of a Lifetime.

Andrew Bernholz had loved baseball since the first time he had picked one up at the age of only five. As his tiny hand came around the lacing of the leather bound ball, he felt something within him ignite. It was like the first moment that a writer picks up a pen or a ballet dancer wears their first slippers. It was like his destiny was chosen from the very first moment that the ball left his hand. He remembered the warm summer day vividly. In fact, it was the happiest memory that he held onto. He and his father played catch in the front yard of their family home. His mother was inside making apple pie and vanilla ice cream, his favorite. His father showed him how to throw a fastball, a wind up, and also, his favorite, a changeup. After that, his father showed him how to bat. He showed him how to get behind the plate, steady his knees, and aim for the back gate. At the time, the back gate was just a tree that was about 5 feet away and in a real field it's about 725 feet away. Andrew worked for the rest of his life to hit the backfield gate. Even though Andrew was a fantastic batter, he preferred pitching, it was his strong suit. There was just something about standing on the mound, with the sun in your eyes, with your hat tipped forward, surrounded by dirt. There was a certain silence that came over the crowd before the pitch happened. There was a certain tension in the air, and Andrew loved every bit of it. He felt like he was on center stage doing something worth watching. Newspapers and bloggers showed up to talk about all of the potential that Andrew was capable of. Coaches from other teams would do everything that they could to convince Andrew to join their teams, including basketball, football and soccer, hoping that his talent would carry over and make their teams as great as the baseball team. Even though he did well at these other sports, no other one would ever take away from his love of baseball. Everything else came second. He learned so many things just from a baseball, a bat, and glove. He learned how to respect his coaches and how to appreciate all of his teammates. The things that he learned on that field would be some of the most important lessons he ever learned.

Andrew spent so many hours of his day standing in front of a return net. He would throw his best ball and it would bounce back to him, ready to try again. Over and over again he practiced different throws, perfecting his pitch. Where the other children saw tedious and obnoxious practicing workouts Andrew saw his nirvana. He would watch as the ball left his hand and made contact in the direct middle of the white taped square that marked the average strike zone. The net would cave under the force that he delivered through the ball. He would critique every spin and each roll, making each and every one better than the last.

After his parents got divorced, when he was only 10, the baseball field was the only place and he had ever felt truly at home. He felt like all the boys in the dugout were his brothers. He felt like the coach was his father. After his father left, he never saw too much of him, maybe once or twice a month. His coach, Randy Watson however, was always around. He would come for late night dinners, bringing mother and him some wonderful food and great company. He would also teach Andrew some great pointers in that same front yard and they would pay catch. They would talk about all of the on goings in school and in life. They would talk about what Andrew wanted to do as he got older. His answer had always been the same: professional baseball player. With the way Andrew played it wasn't a totally irrational dream. In fact, everyone in Greensprings believed that he could do it. He'd been the best to ever play at the high school or at the local college. There was so much determination inside of him; there was nothing that he allowed to stop him. If he wanted to be a professional baseball player then he was going to be a professional baseball player.

That dream had finally begun to become a reality one day in May. Andrew sat on the pitcher's mound, the way that he always had. He adjusted the ball in his fingers so that his pointer, middle and index finger held on tightly but his wrist was loose. The game so far had been what was called a "no-hitter". It only happens when the pitcher strikes out each and every single batter. There was a scout in the audience for the Colorado Rockies. Everyone knew so everyone was playing their best. Still, that didn't stop Andrew from playing the best game of his life. He threw the ball, it flew right over home plate, and the batter didn't swing. The umpire, dressed in a blue polo shirt and khakis, stood up and screamed the best words that a pitcher can hear.

"Strike three! You're out!" The umpire yelled as he stood up and held up his hands.

Andrew's team ran to him, yelling out his name. They picked him up into their arms and yelled with joy. Andrew looked out to the crowd as they cheered and threw their fists into the air. The newspaper took pictures and shouted the headlines that would captivate the entire town. Andrew watched for the reaction of the Rockies' scout carefully. The man that was dressed so well pulled out a cell phone with a smile and called whomever he had needed to. After all of the commotion calmed down, the man came to Andrew. His heart clenched as he got closer and closer.

"How would you like to play for the Colorado Rockies, son?"

Chapter One: A Far Throw

It had been five years since Andrew had been signed to the Colorado Rockies. It had been so long in fact, that it had come for the day for him to retire. That made today his most important game. No pitcher wants to go out losing his last game. Andrew had it in his mind that he was going to throw a perfect game, a game just like the game that got him signed to the Rockies. Andrew focused on the pitch. As he wound up, out of the corner of his eye he caught a glimpse of most beautiful woman he ever seen. She was taller than most women, but she was also the most beautiful woman he had ever seen. Her hair was long and curly. Her face was defined and her body was something to be admired and worshiped. Her dark chocolate complexion seemed to sparkle from the sun. She was jumping up-and-down, holding a sign with Andrew's name. Andrew had not realized it until everyone in the crowd gasped, but he had literally dropped the ball. In confusion, the umpire called it a ball. That put an end to Andrew's perfect game.

 The game ended and people gave their condolences to Andrew. Most people knew how important it had been for him. He walked out the field and began looking for the woman that he had seen, the one that had distracted him from his perfect game. She was the most beautiful woman he had ever seen. He returned to the dugout and sat on the bench. He was going to miss being the center of attention in a huge stadium like this one. When you're a pitcher you wear out your pitching arm exceptionally fast. It's such an unnatural motion for the body to move in, especially on an almost daily basis. Regardless of how much he took care of it the damage had been done. And now, what did he have to show for it? A botched game. Of course, his game had been a victory, just not to the extent that he had anticipated. He pulled his hat over his eyes and looked at all of the sunflower seeds strewn across the concrete underneath the bleachers. He leaned his head back and looked up. Of course, he could always go and watch his teammate's games. He knew the team would move on without him, but he was stuck, stranded without them. His entire life was baseball and now that he didn't have it he didn't know what to do. He felt like he was completely lost. What is one supposed to do after they complete their lifelong dream? He had never really filled his thoughts with anything but baseball before. He had never had any other hobbies or interests, just baseball. The only thought that ever crossed his mind besides baseball was the woman that he'd seen today. He began to think of every way that he could possibly meet her. He was equal parts serious and curious about her. Women threw themselves at him on an almost daily basis. He was used to being the center of attention of models and actresses. He never felt the way about them that he felt about her. She caught his eye, instead of vice versa. He knew that she was a fan; he just had to figure out how to get in touch with his fan.

Andrew had always loved his fans, but he never spent much time with them. He never wanted to chat or talk to them as he signed autographs. That's not to say that he wasn't kind to them, because he very much was. His mind was always just so focused on other things. He knew that without his fans he would have no franchise or career. The thing about professional baseball is that it's just as much about the fans as it is about the talent; although, he didn't have to worry about any of that anymore. Tonight, he would return to his mansion, eat dinner, probably from sort of savory pot roast. Then, he would probably crawl into his bed and wonder some more about what he was going to do with the rest of his life. That was the thought that the news caster was interested in when she brought the microphone to Andrew's mouth.

"I'm sorry, I'm late." She said. "I'm sure you don't want to talk, and I'm sure the bigger stations already got all the good stuff, but, would you mind?"

"I don't mind." Andrew said as he stood up and straightened out his clothing.

"That was some game." The newscaster said with a smile.

"I was distracted." Andrew said, getting a little bit frustrated.

"What was it that distracted you?" The woman asked.

Andrew thought about it. This was going to be the way that he got back in touch with the woman, the way that he reached out to her and got a hold of her. He stood in front of the camera with his back straight.

"Actually, a woman is to blame. She was a beautiful woman. She was wearing one of my jerseys and she had long black hair and the most beautiful eyes that I've ever seen. Any lead on the responsible woman would be highly appreciated." Andrew said with a wink as he gave his number. Almost immediately his phone began to ring.

"Are you serious?" The newscaster asked laughing.

"As serious as throwing the perfect retirement game." Andrew said.

The woman shut off the camera and looked at Andrew.

"Do you know how many replies you're going to get because of that?" She said with a laugh.

"It will be worth it." He said back as he screened calls.

The woman wasn't wrong. It had only been a few hours since Andrew had announced his phone number on live TV and already he had more than one hundred calls. No more would be accepted. Andrew began to call the people that had called him.

Chapter Two: Striking Out

Over 1,000 phone calls came in over the next month. Unfortunately, none of them ended the way Andrew had wanted them to. None of them led him to the woman that had distracted him from the game. He had done everything he could. He had posted on every main social media site, he had returned all of the phone calls, and he had even searched the cameras. He was beginning to give up hope that he was ever going to find the woman again. He was not even sure that she wanted to be found anyway. He was beginning to give up hope when a phone call finally came in.

"Did the woman you saw have dark skin and blue eyes?" The man on the other line asked. Andrew was put off by his old smoker's cough. The man sounded like he was up to no good. Not like he wanted money, just like he wasn't supposed to know about this woman. Andrew couldn't help but to be bit skeptical of the man. He sounded like he was in his late 70's and trying to hide something that he didn't want Andrew to know. Still, he thought that it was worth it to comply. He'd come this far there was no use in stopping it now.

"As a matter of fact she did." Andrew said, intrigued.

"Do you have an email that I can send you a picture of my daughter? I think you may have been talking about her." The man asked. Andrew thought it was a little strange.

"Yes." He replied skeptically. Andrew continued to name off his email address to the strange man. Ten minutes later, he received the picture. It was a picture of a beautiful woman. She had been much younger in the photos than when Andrew had seen her at the game, but it was definitely her. She was absolutely stunning too. She was in a short white summer dress and held a stack of books. She wore a big, beautiful smile on her angelic face. "You said this is your daughter?" Andrew asked in awe that he was looking at her again. He had wanted for so long to see her again, and now there she was on the computer screen, more beautiful than he remembered. As he looked into her deep blue eyes, he realized that he never wanted to look into anyone else's eyes for as long as he lived. She was the vision of perfection and he was willing to do whatever he could to see her again. Unfortunately, that was at the will of the man on the phone. He didn't sound like he was a reasonable man to deal with and this was a sensitive matter, that, if taken into the wrong hands could be easily taken advantage of. Andrew failed to think of any other way that the man could have known about this woman if he hadn't been telling the god's honest truth.

"Yes, that's my little Natasha. That's the last picture I have of her. After she went to college she kind of cut me out of her life. I still know where she is, but I can't go near her. That's where I was hoping that you could come in. I want to get back in touch with my daughter and you can help me with that. If you agree,

I can point you in the right direction of her." The man said. Andrew could tell from his voice that he was being sincere but it was still a strange request nonetheless. He didn't know this man at all, he could be some type of sociopath and not really know her.

"Sir, if you ask me, I think that if she wants you in her life, that she'll let you in her life." Andrew said respectfully, not wanting to upset or anger the old man. He sounded distressed enough. A thousand and one situations ran through his head as to why Natasha would want to keep him out of her life. Andrew's father was known to mess up pretty badly, but never bad enough to where Andrew wanted to kick him out of his life entirely. In fact, he couldn't imagine his father doing something vile enough to warrant such a thing as that. A child's love for their parent is unconditional even when a parent's may not be. Andrew weighed his options.

"Well, what says that she wants you in her life? You went on a national news broadcast about her. I think it's safe to say that neither of us is exactly taking the high road, but I was hoping you'd understand." The man said.

"I'm not a hypocrite, so I guess I'll help you." Andrew said. "What's your plan?"

"She lives in a tiny apartment with her roommates. I can give you the address and then what you do with it is up to you. I just want you to convince her to come back and at least talk to me." The man said.

He gave Andrew the address. Andrew went straight to his computer to confirm it. Sure enough it came back as the home of Natasha Green. Andrew then began to plot and to think about how he was going to woo her. He didn't want it to feel like he just showed up at her house, uninvited. It took him over a week, but Andrew finally had the perfect idea in mind on how to win over Natasha.

Chapter Three: Finally a Hit

Andrew walked up to the small apartment. He heard what must have been at least five women inside laughing and enjoying each other's company. Andrew stood there with a dozen roses hoping that one of them was Natasha. He knocked on the door with a large smile on his face. He held his breath as a woman opened the door. The woman wasn't Natasha, but she was around her age. Andrew smiled as a bewildered look came across her face.
"Is Natasha Green here?" Andrew asked.
The woman's eyes got even bigger. Andrew was dressed in a very expensive suit. He had his hair slicked back, the way that he got the most compliments on it. The woman stuttered as she tried to speak.
 "I'm sorry, she's not here. Who are you?" The woman asked.
"I'm Andrew Bernholz, former Rockies pitcher. Natasha was at my last game. I was hoping that I would be able to speak to her." Andrew answered.
The woman took a moment to gain her mind back before she spoke. She looked down at all that Andrew held.
"I don't think that you're going about it the right way. If you want to speak to Natasha, she's going to be extremely put off by this." The young woman motioned to Andrew from head to toe. "If there's one thing that you need to know about Natasha,

it's that she doesn't enjoy dramatic acts. You're going to have tone it down."

"Thank you for the advice," Andrew said, feeling embarrassed. "Can you please point me in her direction?

"Of course," The woman said. She began to write down the address of a bar on Main Street.

Andrew drove as his stomach clenched into a knot. His heart began to flutter as he watched the bar come into view. He parked his car and walked through the front doors. He sat the roses beside him as he took a seat at the bar. A man dressed in tight pants and a plaid shirt walked up to him.

"What will it be?" The man asked as he cleaned out a glass with a white rag.

"I'll take a rum and Coke, also, can you point me in the direction of Natasha?" Andrew asked. The man looked him over before nodding.

"Here's your rum and Coke. Wait here." The man disappeared behind a curtain. The moments that it took for the curtain to flutter back open made him feel like he waited there for an eternity. Finally, Natasha stepped in front of him. She dropped the tray of glasses that she was holding when she looked at his face.

"Oh my God, Andrew Bernholz, what are you doing here?" She asked.

"Actually, I came here to see you." Her mouth dropped open.

"Are you okay?" Andrew asked.

"Why would you come all the way here just to see me?" She asked with her hands still up to her face.

"Haven't you been watching TV?" Andrew asked.

"I don't have one." She said as she laughed and swept up the broken glass.

"Well, you're the reason why I didn't throw a perfect game. My retirement game, you were there." Andrew said making sure to be as sweet as possible about it. He didn't want to upset her.

"Me?" She said with her eyes wide. "I am so sorry, what did I do?"

"When I saw you I couldn't take my eyes off you. I couldn't keep them on the ball." He said. "Which is pretty much the first rule of baseball."

"Oh, I am so sorry." She said about to cry.

"No, please don't be upset. After I saw you, you're all that I could think about." As Andrew said it, he felt the same overwhelming emotion that took him over when he very first picked up a baseball. She took her hand back and held it to her chest.

"You're not angry?" She asked innocently.

"No, of course I'm not. However, I will be broken if you deny me a dinner date tonight, at the *Blue Moon*." Andrew said with his lady killer grin.

"Of course, I'll go." Natasha said as she looked into Andrew's eyes. Andrew sat at the bar as he enjoyed Natasha's conversation and a few virgin drinks. He admired her astonishing body from her beautiful hair to her large breasts, down to her thick hips and her long legs. Andrew was exceptionally drawn in by her thick, plump lips that he loved to make curl into the most beautiful smile that he had ever seen. He realized that just being able to spend these few hours talking to her was worth it to have missed out on throwing a no hitter for his retirement game. When her shift ended, Andrew drove her back to her apartment so that she could get ready for their date. He frantically called his assistant while he was inside, making reservations for the *Blue Moon* Restaurant. Even men like Andrew had a hard time getting into the restaurant, especially on such short notice, but he put everything that he could into the night. He pulled string after string, and called in favors all because he wanted Natasha to feel what he felt for her.

Natasha came out of her front door looking extravagant. She wore a long red gown that would have dragged the ground if she hadn't kept it in her hand. She wore her long hair into a tight and curly bun that sat on top of her head perfectly. Her makeup had been changed from what she wore before. It was more elegant and sultry. Andrew had finished his call before she glided into the car like the goddess that she was. Andrew admired each and every movement that she danced. He loved the way that she tilted her head back and closed her delightful eyes in joy. It was utterly intoxicating.

Andrew was pleased as they arrived at the *Blue Moon*. He was overjoyed to see that all of his requests had been catered to. The couple had their own waitress and their own balcony table. They sat down, ready to enjoy a gourmet meal. Natasha smiled as Andrew told her all of the wonderful adventures that he had on his journey to becoming a professional baseball player. All of the arrogance that came along with the title that he held drifted away, and it just became an occupation as she listened with her smile.

"How did you find me?" Natasha asked after he finished speaking.

Epilogue: The Perfect Game

"I've been meaning to tell you that, actually. Your father contacted me. He saw the newscast and told me where I could find you." The look that came over her face was perturbed. "Our deal was that he would tell me where you were if I got you to talk to him. "

"I'm not surprised at all that he would do something like that. The reason why I've been estranged from him for so long is because he's an alcoholic. My entire childhood he always talked about how he had a disease. But the truth was that he decided to pick up each and every drink that he saw." Natasha said. Her face contorted into one of sorrow. "He spent the money for my mom's funeral on whiskey."

Andrew understood what it was like to have issues with his parents. He wanted to only make her feel better, but he also wanted to hold up his end of the bargain. He was a man of his word.

"What if he's changed? You don't want to miss that over something that happened in the past do you?" Andrew asked.

"Okay, I guess I do owe him something since he got us together." Natasha said.

After dinner, Natasha directed Andrew to her father's house. It was dilapidated and decaying. A wretched smell came from the house. Andrew held her hand as they walked up to the door. He watched her take a deep breath as she knocked. The man that opened the door was much older than Andrew would have thought that he would be for Natasha's father. He was gaunt, it looked like he had not eaten in almost a month. His skin was covered from head to toe with liver spots. He slouched at an angle, like a large weight had hung across his frail neck for a long time. However, he smiled as he saw Natasha.

"My baby girl!" He yelled as he took his daughter into his arms. At first, she struggled. Then, she eventually wrapped her arms around his thin frame too. "I'm off the hard stuff." He said. Andrew could see the relief in Natasha's eyes as he said it.

"Then why do you look this way, dad?" She asked.

"Drinking is an expensive habit." He answered. A look of shame came across his face while a look of pride came across Natasha's. "I'm sorry Tasha." He said sincerely.

Natasha's father welcomed Natasha and Andrew into his home as he thanked Andrew for holding up his end of their deal. Andrew watched as Natasha began to love, trust and forgive her father again. The sight was beautiful and rare. As Natasha excused herself to the restroom, Andrew sat next to her father who wore a wide smile. His eyes were grateful.

"Sir, I need you to know something. I love Natasha, and I want nothing more than to marry her, but I need your blessing. I see the way that she looks at you and I know that it took a long time, but I know that she cares about you and I know that she cares about what you think." Andrew said. Her father sighed. "Yes. I wouldn't want anyone else more than you to be my son in law Andrew. I'd be honored." He said as he wrapped his arms around him.

Natasha came from the bathroom to see the two of them sitting next to each other laughing. She looked at them with happiness. She had never seen the way that a man was supposed to treat a woman until she met Andrew. Her father had always been too drunk to pay any attention to her mother; if he had maybe he would have noticed her cancer symptoms. She believed that she could find it in her heart to forgive him. She had always believed that he loved alcohol more than her, but, today he proved otherwise.

"Andrew, it's getting late." She said with a smile. Andrew nodded and grabbed his keys before taking Natasha's arm in his and leading her out to the car. Natasha kissed her father goodbye and promised to see him the next day. As they drove, Natasha noticed that Andrew wasn't driving back to the house. He comforted her by telling her that it was a surprise. She watched as they drove out of town and into the parking lot of the Rockies stadium. Andrew opened her door for her as Natasha admired the empty lot and the empty stadium. Andrew pulled out a ring of keys and unlocked the entrance. The two of them walked onto the silent, dark field. All that lit up the sky was the stars above and the full moon. Andrew walked her out to the pitching mound.

"Since I was young this has been my life. It was like the moment I stepped on this mound I was the only person that existed. That changed on that last game. When I saw you it was like you were the only one who existed. I want to exist together." Andrew got down on one knee and pulled out a velvet box. He presented it to Natasha with begging eyes. "Will you marry me Natasha Green?"

"Do you know why I was your fan Andrew?" She asked, taking Andrew by surprise.

"No, why?" He asked.

"Because, you had all this talent, money and power, but I could tell that wasn't what you loved about the game. You were so different than the other men of the field. You loved the game; you were faithful to only a ball, and a bat, not to the women that came with it, or the fame or the cash. I never had a man to look up to in my life but that changed when I saw the very first Rockies game that you played. To see you put this game that you love so much second to me, means so much. So, yes Andrew, I will marry you."

THE END

Printed in Germany
by Amazon Distribution
GmbH, Leipzig